ALWAYS HER MATE

SARAH SPADE

Oh, great. I'm being stalked.

I've only gone two blocks away from Charlie's, the bar where I work, when my inner wolf rouses up from her sleepy doze, instantly alert. She's not snapping or snarling a warning, but yipping sharply to draw my attention to the silent predator padding somewhere behind me.

Poor girl. The two doubles I worked yesterday and today for a distraction must have tired her out if it took her this long to notice. I sensed that he was out there as soon as I stepped onto the street.

He's good, though. I'll give him that. A human would've been oblivious to his presence, a vampire too arrogant to even guess they were being watched, and most shifters wouldn't have noticed the few clues he left behind.

But I'm not most shifters, am I?

At the next crosswalk, I dare a peek over my shoulder while I wait for the light to turn red. Normally, I would just jaywalk—even though the humans in Muncie think I'm just like them, I'm not, and there isn't a single car around fast enough to plow down a shifter—but I take the few seconds to track down where he's hiding.

I snuffle in a breath, but there's no obvious scent over the asphalt, the oil, the garbage, and the stale beer that clings to my Charlie's tee.

Hmm. That makes it a little more difficult.

My stalker is using the mid-August humidity against me. By coming up from downwind, the summer breeze is pushing his scent away from me, giving him an advantage.

Then again, me being an alpha wolf evens the odds, and my nose isn't the only tool I have.

The quick glimpse over my shoulder doesn't tell me much, either. It's late out. Charlie's doesn't really close—it's a supe bar with a majority of vamp patrons who own both the city and the night—but my shift usually ends around eleven or twelve, depending on when it started.

Tonight, I stayed an extra hour later to help Hailey with the midnight rush. I left a few minutes after one, so no surprise that the streets are quiet. Empty. Charlie's is the only place open on this stretch of road, and though my wolf can't pick up on the vamps—she only senses living things and vamps register as dead from their icy skin to their icy, bloody scents—my shifter's sight can see clearly for more than four blocks.

Behind me, I count three vamps making their way downtown. And while the protection I once had against the vamps who run the Fang City is nonexistent nowadays, none of the fangy supernaturals are interested in me.

In fact, once it got out to the local supe community that I'm a shifter—and, not just a shifter, but the fated mate of the Mountainside Pack's Alpha—a majority of the vampires I wasn't already friendly with act is if I don't exist.

I get it. I do. The last thing the Cadre needs is for one of their people to trigger another Claws and Fangs war between shifters and vampires. Right now, our people have an unsteady truce. If I'm forced to defend myself against a rogue vamp, I will, but I'd rather not be responsible for another supe battle if I can avoid it.

The all-powerful Cadre, led by head vamp Roman Zakharov, feels the same way. So even though I gave the charmed fang that shielded me back to my vampire roommate, most Muncie vamps consider me off-limits in one way or another.

And since Roman gave my kinda, sorta, *almost* mate permission to court me inside of Muncie's borders, Ryker gets a pass, too.

Not like he needs one. Ryker's already shown that he'll attack a vampire if provoked. Sure, that vamp happened to be Aleksander Filan, my aforementioned roomie, but still. A powerful alpha wolf himself, Ryker will fight if challenged because, well, we're shifters. That's what we do.

Good thing Ryker's not interested in starting another war, either.

Oh, no. His only aim—as it has been for almost two months, ever since he found me living here back in June—is to convince me to say yes to being his bonded mate. To being his forever, and to rejoining the Mountainside Pack who claim the mountainous territory just outside of Muncie.

I haven't yet, and not only because I'm as stubborn as I am impulsive.

After the last year where I believed that Ryker rejected me, choosing another female to be his mate, I just need a little more time to accept that he wants me for me and not because I'm only the second female alpha that our people have heard of. With the first being our revered goddess, the Luna, it definitely means something that I'm another one.

If only I could figure out *what* it means. Because, yeah. I'm... not so sure yet.

According to pack lore, female alphas have all kinds of tricks up our sleeves. Supposedly, any male she mates with becomes an alpha no matter if he's a beta, delta, or omega when he first lay down with her; if she *bonds* with him, he becomes a god in his own right. And then there's how a single howl ripped from her throat could control any packmate no matter their ranking.

Now, that last one? Yup. I can personally vouch that it's true. As much as I never wanted to use my pack status against another wolf, I did just that during the full moon before last and it totally worked. Which leaves me to wonder about the other rumors.

Wonder? Try obsess.

Since Ryker Wolfson walked back into my life, obsessing has become one of my defining personality traits.

Like now—

I shake my head and, when I see that the light has gone from green to red, I put my hands in the back of my jeans pockets and stroll purposely forward as if I don't have a care in the world—or like I have no freaking idea I'm being followed.

When I left Charlie's earlier, I wasn't in any rush to go home. Why? It's not like I have anyone to go home to.

Six weeks ago, Aleks told me that he needed some space. Even though I haven't officially mated Ryker yet, we're definitely together, getting to know each other and, yes, working our way toward performing the Luna Ceremony that will make us forever mates at last.

Aleks... hadn't taken the news too well.

For months, he'd made it obvious that he was in love with me and that he was willing to wait until I returned his feelings.

And then Ryker showed up in Muncie and that was the end of *that*.

So, yeah. Six weeks ago, Aleks left the apartment that we shared—strictly platonically—and he still hasn't come back. Not to the apartment, and, I'm pretty sure, not to Muncie.

Aside from a single weekly message to let me know he still plans on returning one day soon, he refuses to answer my calls or my texts so I don't really know where he is or what he's doing. It's like he's fallen off the face of the planet, all because he wanted me to choose him instead of Ryker and I couldn't do that.

He told me when he initially left that I was free to stay in the apartment while he went off to clear his head. The stubborn half of me—well, more like *three-quarters* of me—wanted to move out once it became obvious that Aleks was going to be gone for longer than I first thought, but that was something else I couldn't do. He gave me a place to stay last year when I had nowhere else to go. He's trusting me to watch over his apartment which is exactly what I'm going to do.

The apartment is twenty blocks away from Charlie's. That's nothing to a shifter, and I usually choose to walk instead of drive because it helps me burn off some of my wolf's excess energy before I head home to sleep.

With someone matching me step for step, though? Hiding in the shadows, stalking me like I'm some kind of unwitting prey? The twenty blocks might just give them a chance to turn that stalk into a pounce. I'm an alpha. To be reduced to prey is unacceptable to a predator like me.

Good thing I have a backup plan.

Instead of going straight, I turn down the next cross street. If I go down another, then cut over about five blocks, Muncie's urban downtown becomes a little more suburban. There are trees over there. Spots of grass breaking up the continuous asphalt. Townhouses with cute little porches and lawns rather than towering buildings and shop after shop.

It's not where I live, but I've spent some time there lately. Right now, it's the perfect opportunity to try to beat my stalker.

He'll be expecting me to be heading toward my apartment. As soon as I take the cross street, he'll figure out that I've changed up the plan, but that's the best thing about this part of Muncie at this hour of night. If I *do* run into anyone else, they'll either be vamps or humans that are in on our supernatural secret. For once, I don't have to pretend to be what I'm not and, as I turn down the street, I pour on the speed.

I'd go faster if I traded my skin for fur, but that would leave me naked if I have to shift back.

No. Better to stay fully dressed for now.

People always underestimate how fast I am. I guess it has to do with being so delicate-looking and petite; it's the same when I go full wolf, too. Pretty, little blonde girls aren't supposed to be vicious and blood-thirsty. They're certainly not supposed to be able to sprint like they're Usain Bolt.

Once I make it to the main street again, I slow down just enough to pass for human. That burst of speed put some distance between my stalker and me which gives *me* the advantage now. I can either find a spot to hold my ground and confront him, or I can continue toward the townhouse I'm aiming for that's only a couple more blocks away. Either way, it's my decision.

Well, *our* decision.

I ask my wolf. She yips again, reminding me that I'll enjoy it much more if I break for the townhouse, giving the predator at my back something to really chase.

My lips quirk upward in a teeny, tiny grin. My wolf is absolutely right. As I sense him getting closer, I realize that I'll definitely enjoy it more if I let him catch me.

Can't make it *too* easy, though. Where would the fun be in that?

I lope forward, my long blonde hair swaying behind me; in the darkness, the pale color gives him a target. Moving quickly, I'm beginning to think that I might make it to the townhouse after all without being snagged. I still can't scent him, and unless I'm wrong, he seems farther than he should be, like he's decided to back off.

Huh. Not gonna lie. That's disappointing.

I keep going anyway. Since the male who lives in the townhouse isn't supposed to be back again until tomorrow night at the earliest, I'm sure he won't mind if I crash at his place. It's closer than the apartment, I've got a spare key in my pocket that I keep for emergencies, and though I've never been there without him, there's a first time for everything, right?

The townhouse is the third in a row of six. I'm just passing the second when, all of a sudden, my wolf orders me to turn around. A familiar scent fills my nostrils, shivers coursing down my spine as, suddenly, a pair of inhumanly strong arms wrap around my middle and my boobs, trapping my arms at my side. Before I even know what's happening, he's lifted me off the ground, all without so much as a "gotcha".

Luna damn it. I should've realized that such an elite hunter might have gone the longer way around, sneaking up the cross street after letting me think he gave up on the chase.

I should've known better about that, too. He's

proven time and time again that he'll *never* give up where I'm involved.

Because he won't expect anything less from me, I struggle, but I think we both know my heart's not in it; if it was, he'd put me down in an instant. Still holding me tightly, he bends his head just enough to place a warm, welcoming, open-mouthed kiss to the corner of my neck, then moves even faster to carry me the rest of the way to the townhouse.

He must have stopped home before he staked out the outside of Charlie's because he doesn't waste time with a key. He turns the knob, the door pops open, and he easily muscles me inside.

Between his musky scent—of pine and spice and pure unadulterated *male*—and the possessive way he's handling me as if he has every right to, I'm already getting wet. His mouth on my skin only adds to my arousal. And though I'd never admit it to him, there's something about him chasing after me that makes me fucking wild.

In his arms, I'm complete putty. Forget putting on an act that I don't want his hands on me. Right now, I want them *everywhere*. I don't even know if I can wait for him to bring me to the second floor where he sleeps when he can spend a night away from his duties as the Mountainside Pack's Alpha.

Three steps inside of the front room and I'm pretty sure Ryker's thinking the same exact thing as me.

He releases his hold on me, setting me on my feet. He still has me faced away from him, staring at the plain white wall. I have a few seconds to reach behind me before I'm trapped again, his body nestled against mine as if he can't get any closer.

My hands find a pair of tight ass cheeks. *Bare* ass cheeks. Oh, Luna. He's already naked. The bulge I feel digging into my back? Proof that he's as insatiable as ever, and our five-day separation was as hard on him as it was me.

I give his ass a squeeze, then move my hands in front of me again. I lift them until my forearms are pressed against the wall. Arching my back, I push my ass against the hard body caging me in.

Hot breath caresses the back of my neck as he spares a hand to swipe my hair over my shoulder. He goes right to the point where they meet, kissing my skin softly before he opens his mouth again, nibbling.

I want to tell him that he only caught me because I wanted him to. That, if this was a real pursuit, I'd have my claws at his throat for daring to turn predator on me. That I know his nakedness means he'd been tracking me in his fur. That he'd taken an unnecessary risk shifting inside of Muncie all to make the chase more of a challenge—and that he was a cheat.

I never thought he'd go full wolf to play one of our favorite games, and that gave him another advantage.

One thing for sure? I'll definitely remember that for next time.

At least I was right. I figured from the moment I stepped out of Charlie's that Ryker Wolfson had returned to Muncie a day earlier than he had planned to—and that, if I'd gotten to know him as well as I believed I had, the first thing my alpha would want to do was, well, *me*. From the naked body to his hot kisses, it looks like we're on the same page.

Luna, I missed him.

I want to tell him all of that and then more, but all I can let out is a small, eager moan as he lowers his hands, shaping my barely there curves before his fingers reach around to unsnap my jeans.

"I'm sorry, sweetheart," he says in that gravelly voice he uses whenever his wolf is in charge. He might be in his skin, but make no mistake. I'm tangling with a pure alpha right now. "I can't wait any longer to get inside of you again."

"Don't apologize," I breathe out, my own voice catching in anticipation. I've been waiting for this since I first sensed him through our bond. I rub my ass against his erection. "Just do it."

Ryker groans at the friction my jeans create against his naked cock. For a few seconds, he enjoys the sensation before his body stiffens around me.

I know what *that* means. If he doesn't slow down,

he's gonna spurt all over my back before we even get to the good stuff.

I've learned to understand these things about him; not bad for someone who was a virgin barely two months ago. Since we decided to make a go of things, we've not only been getting to know one another—we've also spent countless nights exploring each other's bodies.

I mean, mates should be compatible when it comes to mating, right? I thought so, and it didn't take much to convince Ryker as soon as the full moon began to wane again.

But it's been five days since I've seen him. I guess that's enough to really put him on edge. Unlike when he purposely locks himself up during the full moon, this separation happened during the phase in her cycle when the Luna is waxing. We could've been mating all along if he hadn't had other responsibilities, but now he's back and I'm pretty sure he's about to make up for missing me the last few days.

Pressing my forehead to the wall, I hide my grin.

I can't freaking wait.

2

Using both hands, he yanks my jeans all the way down to the floor.

I'm impressed that, as ruled by the need to mate as he currently is, Ryker actually remembers. After the last time he shredded my jeans in his haste to get to my pussy, I told him that he can either take better care of them or I'll just switch to sundresses again so he'll have easier access to me.

Now, Ryker likes me in jeans. Well, no. He likes me in sundresses. He *loves* me in jeans. He loves Alpha Gem more than the omega I once pretended to be, and he promised he'd refrain from ruining any more of my jeans.

My panties, though? Yeah, the little patience he relied on during his hunt has finally run out. With a quick jerking motion, he tears them off of me. I don't know if he ripped them or he sliced them with a claw or what, but they're gone.

Still grinning, I brace myself.

These days, all it takes for me is to sense Ryker nearby and I'm ready to mate. Lifting my ass, I wait for him to grab me by my hips and hold me steady so that he can mount me.

I should've known better. As desperate as he is, Ryker won't just shove his erection inside of me. He wants me to enjoy sharing my body with him so that I'll finally stop being stubborn and let him be the *only* male who will ever get to fuck me.

Not that he isn't already, but I haven't quite confirmed that fact to him yet. If he wants to work hard to convince me, I'm going to let him, especially when my big shifter drops to his knees behind me, clutching my ass cheeks in his hands as he begins to lick me from behind.

This, uh— *wow.* This is new.

Ryker loves my taste. Since I feel the same about him whenever I take his cock in my mouth, I can't talk, but he'll definitely take any opportunity to eat me out.

Like this, though? Definitely new.

I squeal, rising up on my tiptoes as his licks become a full-on sucking assault on my clit.

"*Ryker!*"

He pulls away long enough to grunt out, "Shirt. Off.

Now," before he's gripping my ass in his big hands, opening me up entirely to his hungry mouth.

I'm using the wall to support my suddenly shaking legs. Pleasure is already spiraling through me, but if Ryker wants me to take off my tank top, it's coming off.

As soon as he sees me reaching for the hem, for once obeying him instead of constantly fighting against him, he goes back to working my pussy with his lips and tongue and, Luna help me, even his canine fangs.

My eyes nearly cross, it's that freaking *good*. I have to take a second to steady myself before I finally rip the tank top over my head, tossing it somewhere behind me. I don't care where. I'll figure that out later when Ryker isn't seconds away from making me come.

Just when I'm on the verge of it, he pulls away, leaving me to snarl a warning at him.

Ryker rises to his feet. He nips my bare shoulder, a rasp of a laugh tickling my skin as he bows his body over mine again.

"Want to come together," he explains as he positions his slick cock against my opening. "You taste so fucking delicious, I just about exploded all over the damn floor. But I want you, Gemma. I need *you*."

I've given up on getting him to call me 'Gem'. He wasn't kidding when he said it was either 'Gemma' or 'sweetheart', but it's all worth it when he goes full alpha and just calls me 'mine'.

Pushing back against him, I take him all the way inside. I'm not worried that he's going to shoot his load in me. It's rare for non-bonded mates to create pups; just like me being a female alpha is super rare, so's the fact that my mom got pregnant by the fated mate she refused to bond with. Besides, he's come inside of me so many times over the last six weeks that, the way I see it, it'll happen if it's going to happen.

And if it does? Maybe then I'll stop worrying that this is all one big dream and that, any day now, Ryker will wake up and decide that he wants to choose another female—or worse, that I'll finally lower my guard enough to finally say yes and he'll turn around and tell me that my submission was all he had ever wanted, but that he'll never be my mate.

See? Told you I was obsessing.

Gritting my teeth, I focus on his cock filling me up, stretching me out as I stubbornly push the terrible, negative thoughts out of my head. He's done nothing to make me think that he's going to give up on me—on *us* —and I'm being freaking ridiculous if I'm obsessing over him changing his mind while he's buried to the hilt inside of me like this.

Ryker is so close to me that he's barely thrusting. Using his hips as a piston, he's rocking quickly, panting softly as he scrapes his fingertips against my naked belly, palms traveling slowly up to my chest.

He shoves my bra up when he hits it, cupping my

bare tits with his massive paws. I can feel the points of his claws poking out, gently needling the tender skin. He won't break it, though. Until I agree to mate him fully beneath the Luna, he won't dare mark my skin. He's saving that for our mating night, but the tiny pinpricks of pain only heighten my desire.

Focus on the now, I tell myself. Don't worry about the future. Don't obsess over what you can't control. Just enjoy Ryker while you have him.

And as he bucks up into me, burying his chin in the top of my hair as he folds himself around me, the two of us coming together... that's exactly what I do.

WE EVENTUALLY MAKE IT TO HIS BED ON THE SECOND floor.

I shed off the last of my clothes while we were still downstairs so now I'm snuggling next to Ryker, skin to skin, enjoying the way his warmth radiates far more effectively than any blanket. I'm pillowing my cheek on one hand, my other arm thrown over his waist, contentedly stroking the dimples in his lower back as he's stretched out on his side.

"I missed you," he murmurs into my neck when he can once again speak in more than snarls and grunts. Ryker nuzzles the hollow of my throat with his nose before swiping it with the flat of his tongue. "I missed you so fucking much."

I love how there isn't even a whisper of deception lurking in his words. He means it, but it's even more amazing to me that he's comfortable enough to tell me.

I smile to myself. "I know."

"You miss me, sweetheart?"

Good question.

Eight weeks ago, we wouldn't be having this conversation because no way in hell would I be lying in bed with Ryker Wolfson.

Six weeks ago, I would've scoffed and lied straight to his face. So what if he could tell? *I* wasn't comfortable then.

Four weeks ago, I would've rolled into Ryker, poked him in his naked chest, and said, "Don't call me sweetheart."

But now? After close to a week's separation, I snuggle closer, moving my hand up his chest until I can press my palm to the five distinct scars that mark the location where his heart is, and sigh.

"Yeah," I admit. "I did."

He places his massive paw over mine. I can feel him rumbling in pleasure, almost vibrating in place. I can't tell if it's because I'm purposely calling attention to his mark, or because I actually told him that I missed him. Knowing Ryker, it's probably both.

"You could've come with me."

"I had work. You know that."

"Mm."

Because *I* know what he's getting at—and that he's *right*—I don't rise to his bait.

Using my job is a cop-out. In so many ways, it's a cop-out. If I asked, Charlie would've given me the week off to attend the annual Alpha gathering. But I didn't ask, and I used my shifts at the bar as an excuse why I couldn't go with Ryker when he left the East Coast five days ago.

The meet happens every year, and families— including intended mates, bonded mates, chosen mates, and pups—are invited to go with their Alpha, so I definitely could've gone with him.

But, even if our relationship status wasn't in flux, there's another reason I should've been there.

Sometime during the end of July, beginning of August every year, all Alphas get together for a large convention-style gathering and, welp, there's my invitation right there. It's a meet for *every* Alpha in the States, and over the last two months, it's gotten out that I'm not just the only female alpha that the American shifters know of, but after I staked my claim to Muncie, I'm technically considered the Alpha of the Fang City I call home.

I didn't mean to do it. Honestly, I'm not so sure *how* I did it. After everything that happened when Shane revealed his true colors—that he was working with my sperm donor, that he wanted to steal me away from Ryker—there's a noticeable division between territories now that can be traced back to that night.

Everything near the mountains that border one side of Muncie belongs to the Mountainside Pack. Ryker's pack. Crossing from the more rural side to the urban sprawl of the city, though, it's not just the vamps that rule this territory.

It's claimed by an alpha wolf shifter. It's claimed by me.

I always teasingly thought of myself as an Alpha of a pack of two, back when it was just me and my vampire roomie, but after the fateful howl beneath the moonlight, I guess my reach went just a liiiittle bit further.

Wonderful, right?

So, yeah, I could've gone to the meet, whether as Ryker's guest or an Alpha in my own right. But that's the thing. *Every* Alpha is invited to the meet and that includes the one wolf that I desperately don't want to face just yet.

Wicked Wolf Walker.

Alpha of the Western Pack, one of the largest and most powerful packs in the country, and my bio-dad—who just so happens to have a huge bounty on my head.

Now, I know that he hasn't gone to the gathering in more than twenty-five years. Not since my mother left him and mated Paul, my adopted father and the Alpha of the Lakeview Pack. Dad—because, until the day I go to meet the Luna, Paul Booker will be the only father I claim—once got the upper claw over the Wicked Wolf and warned him that, the next time, he'd give in to his instincts to slaughter him.

As far as I know, the fight with my dad is the only challenge that Wicked Wolf Walker has ever lost. Since then, he's closed ranks, growing his pack while proclaiming that the Western Pack has seceded from the rest of the United States' shifter community. The dickhead also refuses to answer to any shifter laws and hasn't attended a single Alpha meet for nearly my whole life.

With my luck, though? This would've been the first one he decided to grace with his presence.

I couldn't risk it. And though Ryker didn't know that the Wicked Wolf of the West was my sperm donor until recently, he understood why I wanted to stay away from the gathering even if this thing between us is so new that it was painful to be separated for as long as we were.

"He wasn't there," he says suddenly, as if he can read my mind. Who knows? Maybe he can because he got it right. I'm in bed with him, but my mind is thousands of miles away in the Wolf District of California. "I saw your dad, though. Paul. He threatened to go for my balls if I ever hurt you again."

See? And that right there is why I adore my *chosen* dad.

"They say that the Wicked Wolf never bluffs. But my dad? Believe me. He might seem like a nice guy, but I grew up sparring with him. He taught me how to fight. He'd have your nuts on a necklace and you singing like a soprano before you even shifted."

Ryker chuckles, squeezing my fingers gently. "He teach you to go for the heart, too?"

"He taught me to make an impact," I shoot back. "I couldn't go for your dick because I had plans for it. But when I thought you gave your heart to someone else, that's what I aimed for. You're just lucky I didn't rip it out."

I had been close. Furious, embarrassed, and dealing with a broken heart of my own, I straddled this male, my claws jabbed into the meat of his chest, and really thought about yanking that sucker out. But I didn't, and I'm glad my wolf talked me out of it since I would've regretted never getting the chance to love him.

Ryker slips his thumb under mine, circling my palm.

His claws are gone, I notice, as he says almost solemnly, "No, sweetheart. I'm lucky that you gave me another chance after I fucked up with the whole Trish thing."

Even though I'm comfy, cozy, and well-boned, just

hearing Ryker say that name has some of my post-coital bliss wearing off.

I try to cover my sudden unease up with a tease. "Really, Ryker? This is your idea of pillow talk?"

I just... I know what Ryker was trying to do last year. As much I hate it, I understood after he finally explained himself. Trish Danvers had been black-mailing him, using the fact that she knew that I was a female alpha to keep him from officially mating me when I first arrived in Accalia. She wanted him, and she was willing to do whatever she had to to get him.

It wasn't anything personal. Not really. Any female who got in her way would've been a target, and the fact that I was Ryker's fated mate—confirmed by the Luna herself—made her despise me. When Shane gave her the proof she needed to try to convince Ryker to choose her instead, she must've thought she hit the freaking jackpot. So determined to keep my secret for me, Ryker decided to play along until he could figure out how she'd gotten that proof—and who she was working with since it was obvious she wasn't doing it alone.

Turned out, it was Ryker's "devoted" Beta, Shane, who had done everything he could to throw Trish at his Alpha. Not because he thought they were a good match or anything, but because he was also aware that I was a female alpha and, instead of blackmailing

Ryker, he used the information to try to convince me to mate *him*.

He even went so far as to plant the idea in my head that Ryker really did choose Trish and that he was stringing me along. I believed him, and when Ryker went ahead with his plan to hold off on our mating until he got to the bottom of what was going on in his pack, I walked out on him.

Well, no. I threatened to rip out his heart, had to hear him tell me that I was nothing to him, and tore out of the Alpha's cabin like a bat out of hell.

So, you know. Po-ta-to, po-tah-to.

Ryker's a born alpha himself. He thought he knew what he was doing. At the very least, he figured he could make me understand—but then I drove my Jeep out of Accalia and by the time he was ready to come after me, I'd met Aleksander Filan and started my new life in Muncie.

For a year, Ryker couldn't find me, all thanks to Aleks's help. Of course, I had no freaking clue at the time that he was even searching for me, or that Aleks's feelings for me had the vampire claiming me as his future mate long before I even knew he cared for me as more than the stray he brought home with him.

Now I do, and now I also know that Trish wasn't working against Ryker. She just really wanted to be his mate. Out of some sick, twisted form of affection, she tried everything she could to get him to choose her.

Shane, though? Shane *was* working against him. Even worse, he was working with my psycho sperm donor to take down Ryker and get to me.

Shane Loup wants to be an Alpha. To do that as a born beta wolf, he needs to mate an alpha female. He needs to mate *me*.

Yeah. Good luck, asshole.

But just like Ryker loses his shit whenever anyone mentions his former Beta—who is currently the Beta of the Western Pack, according to Ryker's intel—I can't get over how much Trish Danvers bothers me. Even if the pretty brunette shifter isn't so evil as to have been involved in Shane's scheme, she still tried to take Ryker from me. I... I can't forgive that.

Knowing that he kicked her out of the pack a month and a half ago helps, but not all that much. She's a chink in my armor, a weakness that I wish I could get over, but I *can't*. And Ryker knows it.

Lifting my hand to his lips, he kisses my knuckles softly.

I love this side of my fierce, rugged alpha. Usually, he's either cold and in control, or bristling with rage as his wolf comes to the forefront. Only when it's the two of us alone together, vulnerable and close, do I get to see the Ryker that stole my heart when I was just a kid.

"You're right. I shouldn't have brought her up."

Ugh. And now he's being so understanding, too? It's like he wants to fall even deeper in love with him.

3

I shake my head. "No. I'm not. I'm being a bitch. Sorry... if you can laugh over me trying to rip out your heart, I should be able to deal with the whole Trish thing now that I know the truth. Especially since you promised me no more secrets."

Ryker shifts his head so that his dark gold gaze is locked directly on me. In the depths of his eyes, I see the same promise he made to me at the beginning of our courtship. He'll remember that I'm an alpha and that he doesn't get to make decisions for me, just like I'll remember that *he's* an alpha and, sometimes, it'll be inevitable.

Just like us.

"No more secrets. From the moment we first mated, we're in this together, Gemma. We're partners."

I love you.

Oh. I almost say the words. In fact, I cough, choking them back so that I don't.

I won't say them first. I absolutely refuse. For all of Ryker's posturing about how we're partners, about how we're fated, about how we're mates even if we're not officially bonded yet, he's never told me he loves me. And, until he does, I can't say yes to him even if I really, really want to.

I almost did during the last full moon. For three weeks, Ryker courted me, spending as much time in Muncie as he dared to now that Accalia is missing its Beta. We went on dates, walked the length of the city together, went on runs in our fur that always seemed to end up with us fucking in its only park. I swallowed my pride and let him cook for me. Then, when I realized that Ryker was amazing in so many ways but he was a shit cook, I made dinner for him.

By the time the full moon came around, I was ready to say yes. But for all the talks we had, all the deep conversations we shared, hopes for the future, reminiscing about the past... our feelings for each other never came up. And maybe he's just assuming that I know that he loves me. Ryker's not the kind of guy who uses words when actions speak so much louder.

But sue me. I need the freaking words.

So, last month, Ryker allowed his trusted pack council—all vetted by him after Shane's shocking betrayal—to lock him in his basement. He point-blank ordered them to keep me away from him, even going so far as to send a pair of wolves into Muncie to guard me while he couldn't.

I have no idea what he promised the Cadre to allow Dorian and Jace to pace outside of my apartment building in their fur, but they spent the whole full moon watching me while I spent it with the old standby: my vibrator and a half-gallon of Breyer's.

Right now, the Luna is in her first quarter phase, halfway between the new moon and the full moon. I have plenty of time until I have to worry about what's going to happen when she's out again at the end of August, but these last few days when he was gone made me realize just how much I really did miss him.

The whole last year, I couldn't let myself. This past week, I did. I missed him, but I'm nothing if not stubborn so I swallow back the "I love you" until he's ready to tell me first.

I don't know why I bother. I'm pretty sure that I blew up my spot that first time together with him. So mindless with lust and the overwhelming sense of pleasure as we mated under the growing moon, I told him that I loved him more times than I should've, but he never said the same then or since.

I try not to dwell on that. Even if it takes him longer to say them, that's okay. We've only been... dating, I guess?... dating for two months. Being fated mates makes everything different since it's just assumed that, sooner or later, we'll love each other. Maybe I'm just impatient. Could be. I really don't know.

One thing I do know, though? Being with Ryker is worth the wait.

"I'm good with that," I tell him honestly. "Being partners. We're a good pair." Slipping my hand out of his hold, I tap his chest. "Just don't go away for so long again, okay? I don't like missing you."

His smile is breathtaking. Even with the dark stubble covering his sharp jaw and his sculpted features, his smile is one of the sexiest things about him. Probably because it isn't often that the protective alpha is relaxed enough to show it off.

But he can be with me.

"I came back a day early," he points out.

That's true. I wasn't expecting him until tomorrow night which was why it was such a surprise to sense him stalking behind me.

"But you were still gone for five days. Do you know how much trouble I could've gotten into in five whole days? Who knows? I might've even forgotten that you existed."

Ryker knows I'm teasing. The only way I can get away with ribbing him is because he can tell that I'm not being honest. Even if me and Ryker don't work out, I know that they'll never be another male for me. Ever. Cheating? Shifters are wired to be loyal, which is just another reason why my sperm donor is unlike any wolf I've ever met. He slept with anything female in his pack; it's the only way my mom avoided being bonded to him because, once he chose her and they performed the Luna Ceremony, they'd be mated for life. A fate worse than death for a sleazy sex addict like Wicked Wolf Walker.

Like me, Ryker was a virgin when we mated the first time. Because, like me, he's known for more than eleven years that I was his fated mate and he was loyal to the idea of us even before the Luna announced that we *were* fated. And, like me, he'll wait until it's the right time for us to make it final.

Until then, we'll have a lot of fun getting closer and practicing the physical act whenever we get the chance.

Between his responsibilities as pack Alpha and my job down at Charlie's, we don't often get to be alone together this long and, if only for a moment, I'm going to savor it.

I can also feel that he's hard again. His wayward cock is nudging at my hip, though Ryker seems just as content to simply hold me.

No surprise that's he's already recovered; I've learned that a shifter's libido is only matched by our stamina. Even though he's already come twice tonight, he's probably ready for another round.

Know what? So am I.

I'm just about to rise up and straddle him when, suddenly, Ryker grips me by the chin. "What if I tell you that I brought something back with me?" he rasps out, his throaty voice gone husky. "Will you forgive me for leaving if I give you your gift?"

"A present?" My eyes light up. "For me?"

I grew up an only child. As an alpha, I was a handful, and though my mom and dad always talked about having other pups, it just never happened for them.

My Aunt Corinne, my dad's sister, has twin boys: Devin and Max. They're both deltas and the closest thing to siblings that I have. A year older than me, they grew up believing I was an omega like my mom and their mom. They were as overprotective as my dad, coddling me since I was the only girl in the family. It didn't matter that I was Paul's adopted daughter. I *was* family. And, okay, I was pretty damn spoiled, too.

So a gift? That's a huge part of my love language. I can wait for Ryker to say the words, but just knowing that he thought of me and brought me back a gift? That gets me right in the chest.

Sex can wait. I want my present.

I hold out my hand. "Gimme and I promise I'll forgive you."

Ryker chuckles again, pinching my chin before he scoots away to climb out of the bed. I must've been right before when I guessed he'd already stopped by the townhouse because he heads right to his dresser, pulling a small, brown jewelry box out of the top drawer.

Hmm. Boldly telling myself that sex can wait might've been a little hasty there, Gem. I'm not so sure what deserves my attention more: the box cradled in his palm, or the gorgeous erection jutting from between his thick thighs.

Decisions, decisions...

Then Ryker plops the box into my outstretched hand and I decide that I'll get to his cock in a second.

Yeah. Present first.

"Thank you."

A quick scowl forms on his handsome face. "Don't thank me. Bringing my mate a present is the least I can do."

He likes to refer to me as his mate, as if he thinks that, if I hear it enough times, eventually it'll just be true.

This time, I let it go. I'm not going to argue with him when I've got his gift in my hand, his jizz in my pussy, and his scent all over every inch of my skin.

Instead, I open the box, another *thank you* halfway to my lips if only because I know it'll needle Ryker and, okay, it's fun to needle him. But then I peek inside, and the bedroom light glints off of the golden chain nestled on the bed of cotton, and my words get caught again.

But it's not the chain that's made me speechless. It's

the familiar-looking charm hanging off the middle of the chain that has me gaping at his gift.

It's not a real fang. Not like the fang that Aleks gave me, and that I abandoned back in the apartment with him. It looks like one, though. Just shorter. Thicker. Still, it's a canine—a *canine* fang.

Ryker's canine fang.

Oh, Luna.

I don't have to ask what this is. Though I recognize the fang as Ryker's, and it's cast in gold instead of being a real tooth, it's so clearly a replacement for the charmed fang that Aleks gave me more than a year ago that I don't know what to say.

Somehow, "What the fuck were you thinking?," probably won't go over too well.

I'll be the first to admit that I'm still jealous over the relationship—even if there never really was one— that he had with Trish Danvers. But that? That's nothing compared to the rivalry between Aleks and Ryker.

It doesn't matter that I told both males that, if I have to, I'll always choose Ryker—and this necklace proves it.

"Um. Thank you," I tell him again. This time, I'm not even trying to needle him. I just honestly can't think of anything else to say.

His dark gold gaze goes bright like brilliant molten lava as he peers down at me. He's still

standing at the side of the bed, the lamplight silhou-
etting him, and I can sense the anticipation coming
off of him in waves when he asks me, "Aren't you
going to put it on?"

Since I also can't think of any valid reason why I
shouldn't, I gingerly lift the necklace out of the box.
Dropping the box onto the bed, I unclasp the chain,
loop it around my neck, and fasten it. The golden
canine settles against my chest.

It's so much heavier than Aleks's fang, and I refuse
to read any symbolism into that.

"It looks good," I say, patting it.

Nope. Still weighs a freaking ton.

"I had it made for you special, sweetheart. I figure,
since you gave up the parasite's fang, maybe you'd
rather wear one of mine. You know. A fang from the
male that has a right to claim you."

I almost point out that I had no idea what wearing
Aleks's fang meant until Ryker explained it to me. I
always believed that it was a mark of protection, that
the other vamps in Muncie would know that I was
protected by one of their own.

How was I supposed to know that it meant that
Aleks thought of me as his mate?

Something tells me that that's the wrong way to
react to his gift, though.

So, rather than bring up Aleks, I just say, "I appreciate it, but if any vamp in Muncie sees this, it won't do

the same thing that a vamp fang does. The gold will give it away."

Because vamps mark their mates—and prospective mates—with a pure fang, snapped right from their gums. They can do that since their regenerative properties regrow their fangs. I'm not sure if it'll work the same way for a shifter, but I guess Ryker didn't want to find out.

Or he wanted it to be gold on purpose. So that it *can't* pass as a vamp fang.

Yeah. I'm going with the second option, especially when Ryker says, almost off-handedly, "I still want you to wear it for me. But if you don't think it'll help keep you safe in the Fang City, maybe it's time you give it up."

"The necklace?"

"No, Gemma. Muncie."

And... there it is. I'm actually surprised it took this long into our time together tonight for him to bring it up.

I pull myself into a sitting position. Now that the conversation has taken this turn, I'm pretty sure more sex is off the table.

Gee, I wonder why? I guess something about Ryker trying to push up against my personal boundaries *again* just totally rips me out of the mood.

Even though I know what he's going to say, I play my role to perfection; I guess, in some ways, I'm still an actress at heart. "Gee, Ryker. If I can't live in Muncie anymore, wherever will I go?"

He knows I'm being disingenuous on purpose, but he's determined and he's opened up this can of worms and Luna knows that nothing is going to stop him from trying to get his way.

"You can come with me." He moves around to my side of the bed, leaning down to cup my face in his hands. "Come home."

But that's the problem. Accalia isn't my home. Pack territory isn't my home. Right now, Muncie is.

I haven't been back to the mountains in six weeks —and for good reason, too. I still have nightmares involving the black hoods Ryker's packmates wore the night they poisoned me with mercury and threw me to the mercy of a chained, feral alpha wolf.

I've never told him the precise details of what happened during that full moon. He knows in general what went down: how I followed our bond to the Alpha cabin, met Audrey, she put mercury in my Coke, then Ryker's pack council presented me to him because they believed that, as his intended mate—his *fated* mate—I should just bond with him already.

It's the little things I kept secret. The hoods, for one. How terrified I was when the mercury kicked in and I was cut off from my wolf. How, as an alpha, I was used to being in charge, and his packmates made me feel weak.

I *hate* that they made me weak.

My wolf wants revenge. Going back there won't be good for anyone until I can forgive the Mountainside Pack for what they did to me otherwise my wolf will push me to after it.

Not poor Audrey, though. Of them all, I've forgiven her, even if she was the one who gave me the doctored drink. All she had wanted was for her pack to have its Alpha couple, and I can understand that. I don't have to like it, but I can understand it.

But her brother is Shane Loup, the former Beta who betrayed the whole pack. Instead of siding with him after his betrayal came to light, she stayed behind, proving her loyalty to her Alpha while she cut ties with her traitorous brother. For that alone, I can forgive her.

I still want to smack her mate, Grant, though.

And Ryker really thinks I'll be happy up on the mountains? No job? No friends? No independence? Just the status of Ryker's mate?

Maybe that's what other shifters want out of life. Maybe that's what *I* wanted when I was still pretending to be Omega Gem. But not now. Not now that I know better.

I shake him off. He lets me, stepping back as I climb out of the bed. His gaze dips, running over my naked body before his eyes land on his necklace again, but I don't care.

He laid down with an alpha wolf. Now he's about to go nose to nose with one.

Once I've put a few feet between us, I perch my hands on my hips, giving him one hell of a daring look.

"Speaking of the pack," I say, purposely changing the subject, "have you found a new Beta yet?"

Ryker's eyes snap to mine. His nostrils flare, his jaw going tight.

And, oof. I regret asking that almost immediately.

Impulsive Gem strikes again.

Bringing up Shane's betrayal is one surefire way to make Ryker bleed without using my claws. Not only because he's furious with himself for not seeing what was under his nose the whole time, but because he has to deal with the knowledge that his trusted Beta made a move on his intended mate.

Of course I know that Mountainside doesn't have a true Beta. Like alphas and omega, betas aren't as common as you would think. Most packmates are a mix of deltas and gammas and, as such, most of his inner circle are delta wolves. Though he's sure he can trust the other seven members of his pack council, none of them are betas so none of them can fulfill that open spot in the pack's hierarchy.

His father's old Beta had stepped down when Henry Wolfson had his accident more than a year and a half ago. For now, he's slipped back into the role, but only until Ryker finds a replacement.

So, yeah. Sore subject all the way around.

And because, deep down, Ryker is as jealous an alpha as I am, he immediately turns around with a low blow of his own.

He crosses his arms over his bare chest. "Filan."

I tense. "What about him?"

"You're still waiting for him to come back. That's why you won't move back to Accalia. Why you insist on staying here. You want him to come back to you."

That's not just low. He's scraping the basement with that one.

"Don't you dare, Ryker. Don't you dare try to pull this shit on me."

His jaw clenches. "Yes or no, Gemma. Answer the question."

He wants to do this? Right now?

Fine.

"Then no. I'm not."

He whooshes a breath out through gritted teeth. "You're lying."

I am. Of course I am. I told Ryker what he wanted to hear, and I hoped he would accept it and just let it go. We don't need to have this fight—*again*.

Still, I'm not even a little surprised that he called me out. If Shane can be believed, it's an alpha thing, being able to sense when someone else is lying. I've always been able to myself, but it wasn't until I really started to spend a lot of time around Ryker that I realized that he can tell, too.

But only when it's a bald-faced lie. That's how Shane was able to trick the both of us. He never actually *lied* lied until the night he helped me escape a feral Ryker suffering from moon fever and tried to sell the whole Trish and Ryker story hard. He was lying, but it didn't matter that I knew. He was ready to reveal his true colors that night and he did.

Before that, he must've been careful to twist his words. Aleks was able to do something similar. He made me think what he wanted me to, and it wasn't until Ryker showed up that I discovered just how much Aleks was hiding from me in the hopes that I would eventually fall in love with him.

I love him, but I'm not in love with him. I *am* waiting for him if only because I'm not just going to leave Muncie without seeing him again. I thought Ryker understood that.

Guess not.

"You wanted me to trust you when it came to Trish," I remind him, "but you won't do the same for me."

"He's in love with you."

I raise my eyebrows. "Are you telling me that Trish wasn't in love with you?"

I hate it when Ryker brings up Trish. But Ryker? He hates it just as much when I throw her in his face.

Oh, well. He deserves it.

"That's not the same thing and you know it."

"Mm-hmm."

"Gemma..."

I bat my eyes up at him. "Yes?"

His growl is a rumble deep in his chest. His claws are still out when he stabs his pointer finger at me. "Now, don't you pull that shit on me."

"Don't like it when I play your game, do you, Ryker?"

"Damn it, Gemma, this isn't a game!"

Nope. It isn't. Because if it was? I'd be having a lot more fun than I currently am. Especially since I'm naked, Ryker's naked, and there's a whole big, empty bed behind us.

Earlier, I needed a distraction to keep me from dwelling on how much I missed him, so I pulled a thirteen-hour shift at the bar.

Our nakedness and the allure of that bed? They're the types of distractions I *don't* need.

Reaching around him, I snatch the comforter, yanking it from the bed before wrapping it around me.

Ryker sucks in a breath, his cheekbones seemingly jutting out from his face at the force of it. "What are you doing?"

"What does it look like? I'm getting ready to leave."

"I thought you were going to spend the night."

No. He expected that he would bone me into

unconsciousness and then I'd fall asleep in his arms. Even though I always head back to my apartment at some point during the night when he's in town, Ryker always insists that I stay.

But I don't. I can't. I'm not sure if it all started our first night together when I left him beneath the Luna or if it's my inability to truly accept that he's choosing me, but I'm always gone by morning and he knows that.

Did he think the fang would change my mind? If so, he has another think coming.

I turn away from him. "I'll see you later, Ryker."

"I'm going back to Accalia in the morning," he calls after me. "But this conversation isn't over. If I can get away, I'm coming back tonight and we *will* discuss this, Gemma."

Huh. We will, will we?

Okay. I know it's immature. I know I'm choosing to walk away instead of talking this out like a respectable female.

Oh, well.

I shoot my middle finger in the air and storm the rest of the way toward the stairs.

4

My wolf snaps at me as soon as we step outside of Ryker's territory.

It doesn't matter that I can sense him. That, on the other end of our strengthening bond, I can *feel* him. She's just majorly pissed that I'm walking away from him when his wolf, like usual, tried to compel us to stay.

She wants me to turn around, to march back inside of that door, and to finally turn Ryker's rented townhouse into a den for the two of us. No surprise. Even though he's never come out and *said* it—Luna forbid Ryker actually explain himself to anyone unless he has to—that's exactly what he's trying to do.

First, a den for us in Muncie, then a cabin together in Accalia. He has our life together all planned out. All he's waiting for is for me to fall in line.

But I can't do that, either. I have an apartment of my own, responsibilities of my own, a *pack* of my own —and, until I make up my mind one way or another about Ryker, I can't stay in his rented place any longer than I already have.

I glance back at the front of the townhouse, inwardly snap at my wolf to settle down, then shove my hands in the back pockets of my jeans as I march away from him. Before I stormed out of the front door, I had only stopped long enough to yank on my tank and my jeans. He's probably not gonna be happy when he sees I left my bra and panties behind, but I had to bolt if only because it rubbed my wolf the wrong way that the stubborn alpha didn't come rushing after us.

He did the same thing the night I first left Accalia. Instead of chasing after me, he stayed behind with his pack council. And, sure, I know that he was covering up for me when my hotheaded actions put my alpha nature on display, but by choosing to stay, I disappeared from Accalia—and then I didn't see him again for a whole freaking year.

That won't happen again. I'm not going anywhere, and as soon as we both cool off, he'll track me down again. I'm sure of it. And, this time, there's nowhere I can hide from him.

As I stomp down the street, I can feel the weight of his canine nestling between my boobs. The fact that I didn't rip it off and throw it at him should've been enough for him for now, but it's not. Nothing I do is good enough, and I know exactly why.

Ryker Wolfson won't be satisfied until he owns every single part of me.

He'll do anything in his power to make it so. Between surprise appearances at my job, mind-blowing sex, making me food, and bringing me gifts, he's using every tool in his arsenal to get me to agree.

And I'm close. So, so close to giving in.

The guy splits his time between taking care of his pack and courting me, like they're both his full-time jobs. Luna, he even turned a vamp city townhouse into another Alpha cabin for him since, no matter how many times he offers, I'm still too stubborn to return to the mountains with him.

Once Ryker accepted that my elusive *yes* might take longer than he thought, he realized that he would need a place of his own in Muncie. It would take too much time to travel back and forth between Muncie and Mountainside during the time he wanted to designate as "ours". Plus, there was the whole "Gem living with a bloodsucker" thing. No matter what went down between me and my vamp roomie, I draw the line at inviting Ryker inside of Aleks's and my apartment.

There's no reason for him to enter my territory. We have his townhouse if we need privacy, and before he arranged to rent it? We already proved that we could mate pretty much anywhere. The shadowed areas of the park. The abandoned trails in the woods surrounding Muncie. The backseat of my jeep when I purposely park it out of sight of prying eyes. Even, one memorable time, up against the brick wall behind Charlie's.

But in the apartment I share with Aleks? It just... it doesn't seem right. And even though this thing between me and Ryker has been exclusive for more than two full moons now, I still can't bring myself to closely examine the reasons *why*.

Luckily, my calculating Alpha ran the numbers and decided that, if I was stubbornly clinging to my life in Muncie, he might as well be comfortable. With the blessing of Roman Zakharov—the head vamp in the Fang City, and the leader of the mysterious Cadre that controls Muncie—he's allowed to rent a townhouse near the bar where I work.

To my surprise, I later found out that Ryker got permission—another shock, I gotta admit, since alpha wolves *never* ask for permission—to both court me and make this place his own at the same time.

Right after the brutal fight between Ryker and Aleks down at the bar, Ryker used his status as my intended mate to get Roman to side with him instead of Aleks. So, when he's not at Mountainside, either doing his Alpha duties or trying to deal with the fall-out from Shane's betrayal, he's usually here.

When he first tracked me down, he devoted as much time as possible to convincing me to return to the pack with him. I quickly put an end to that. I might be willing to see if what we have is something I'll eventually make permanent, but after suffering the sting of his rejection this past year, I just can't jump into a forever mating paws first.

Besides, this is just another stage of the mating dance. We're getting to know each other—the real Ryker and Gem, not the aloof Alpha and Omega we appeared to be—and testing out the waters of a prospective mating without actually bonding first.

I know that Ryker wants me to just say yes. It would be so easy to. Say the word and perform the Luna Ceremony and we'll be together forever.

Only... the last year has fucked me up. No matter how happy this male makes me, there's a tiny part of me that's convinced that it won't last. That something's going to come along and ruin what we have. Ryker could reject me again, or his traitor of a Beta might stick his snout in where it doesn't belong, and I know that Trish Danvers was kicked out of the pack six weeks ago, but what if she comes back?

Excuses. They're all excuses. I know it, and when Ryker lets his frustrations out, he tells me that he knows it, too.

But he accepts it anyway because, after all, it's my choice. A mate has to choose.

And I'm choosing to wait just a little longer.

It's not like I'm the only one who's ever made an Alpha wait, either. Sure, our shifter rituals say that an Alpha couple should be installed as soon as possible after a new Alpha takes over the pack; that's why I was first sent to mate Ryker last year, after his father's accidental death. There's precedent for waiting, though. Paul Booker, when he took over the Lakeview Pack, decided that he wouldn't even ask the Luna for the name of his fated mate. He would run his pack as Alpha, and if he found a mate that he chose, then great. He wasn't going to be trapped into a forever mating just because it was expected of him and, as the Alpha, he had the authority to change the rules as he went along.

Of course, a few years into being Alpha, he met my mom and chose her. But even there there's precedent. Instead of bonding herself to him their first full moon together, she got to know him, got to respect him, even trusted him enough to tell him my secret, and only then did she bond with him six months later.

And don't get me started on my mom and my bio-dad. Wicked Wolf Walker acted as her mate for three years, though they never bonded. My mom avoided him every time the Luna was out, and he pointedly didn't push the topic of the Luna Ceremony if only because—once he was fully bonded—he wouldn't be able to sleep with every damned female in the Western Pack.

It's just... Ryker doesn't want to wait anymore. He hasn't wanted to wait since he came back into my life, claiming me as his. But until I say yes and accept him? That's all he can do.

I understand why Ryker's so eager to cement our bond. Even though we've only been *together* together for a little less than two months, he's known that I was his mate just as long as I've known he was destined to be mine: *eleven years*. He's lived his life with the aim of making me his bonded mate and now that he can? Now that he's an Alpha ready to give Mountainside its Alpha couple? I'm the one putting my foot down.

And what sucks so bad? Is that I *know* I'm sabotaging the one thing in life I've always wanted. Eleven years, I looked forward to staking my claim to Ryker Wolfson.

So why the hell am I fighting so hard against it?

Ugh.

Frustration pulses through me. I lash out, kicking the nearest lamppost, wincing when my shifter strength has the metal pole snapping.

Whoops.

The post comes crashing down, hitting the asphalt with a smash. Broken glass tinkles, the faint light blinking out as I break into a flat-out sprint before anyone can blame me for the destruction of city property.

I blame my guilt over smashing the lamppost for what happens next. Too consumed with fleeing the scene of my crime, I stopped paying attention to my surroundings. Though the Cadre runs Muncie, there's still a pretty healthy human population inside its borders. Humans mean cops. I keep expecting one of the boys—or girls—in blue to pop up out of nowhere, pissed off that the lamppost is broken, and puzzled that a tiny thing like me could be responsible for the mess.

If I get arrested for vandalism, no way that won't get back to the Cadre—or Ryker. I can just hear the lecture now. Impulsive Gem, so reckless that she showed off her shifter strength in public.

No, thanks.

But while I worried over a human coming after me, I totally forgot that there are plenty of other dangers in Muncie, especially for a shifter like me. Not every vamp is a fan of Aleks, and even if Roman okayed me moving to Muncie, I'd be a fool to think the vampires in the Fang City are happy I'm here. There's the Nightmare Trio, for one, who would've eaten me if Aleks hadn't stopped them, and they're not the only ones who'd love to take a bite out of me.

Aleks's charmed fang didn't just mark me as his and offer me his protection. Oh, no. Whatever he did to it, it covered up my scent so that none of the other supes in the city could tell that I was a shifter.

Without it? It's obvious what I am. My scent gives me away. Right now? I'm loaded with shifter pheromones. There's also my inherent scent and Ryker's musk mingling on my skin, and it's strong enough to attract any vamp up to no good.

Like the pale-skinned, dark-haired male that suddenly steps out in front of me.

I stop short, immediately dropping into a crouch.

I've spent my whole life living amongst predators of one kind or another. There's something about the way he sizes me up that tells me that he's not going to be one of the vampires that goes on his merry way, pretending I don't exist. He's looking for a fight, and he's found me.

Plus, the way his eyes are already blazing blood-red kind of gives me a clue that this one is definitely up to no good.

His upper lip curls, revealing a set of vamp fangs nearly two inches long. "Wolf."

I snort. "Asshole."

His eyebrows wing up. "Excuse me?"

I lift one shoulder, then let it fall. A half-shrug. "Sorry. I just thought we were stating the obvious."

"You're cute," he drawls. "For a mangy mutt, at least. Filan thought so, too. Maybe now that you've run him off, I'll take a turn and see what it is about you that's so special."

Oh, Luna. That was probably the worst thing this vamp could say to me right now.

The obvious threat is bad enough. Fucking perv vamp, I'm going to enjoy kicking his ass for that alone. But to throw in my face that I'm the reason Aleks is gone?

I don't give a shit if that's true. I'm gonna make him pay for reminding me anyway.

I crack my hands, releasing my claws. Slowly, I rise from my defensive crouch, preparing to go on the offense.

With a smile, I say sweetly, "You can *try*," right before I attack.

───────

I DON'T KILL HIM, EVEN IF MY WOLF IS TOTALLY ON BOARD with me doing just that.

I'm a shifter. As a vampire, the undead supe is my natural enemy. I've managed to sideline most of my urges since I made Muncie my home, but this prick got me on the wrong day. I was already so worked up after how I left things between Ryker and me, and then I had to deal with some hotshot vamp taunting me over Aleks?

No fucking way.

Once again, I use my appearance to my advantage. That, and the vampire race's tendency to be super arrogant. He never expected that I'd use my claws to rip him a new one, but I do, and by the time he's prepared to fight back, I've already left him bleeding in so many places, he'll need to tap a vein or two before he can even think of fighting back.

I'll give him credit. As cocky as he seemed to be, he knows his limitations. My size and fearlessness caught him off guard, giving me the advantage, but once he can finally get out from under my angry claws and snapping jaws, he bolts. He obviously thought that his being a vamp would be enough to subdue me. After underestimating me, he takes the first chance he gets to take off into the night.

Doesn't mean he won't come back with either reinforcements or after he's had a refill.

Yup. Time to get out of Dodge while the going's still good.

Since I absolutely refuse to destroy these jeans after the lengths Ryker went to earlier tonight to save them, I don't shift. I do, however, sprint the rest of the way back to my apartment.

I'm coated in blood. Barely any of it is mine, and a shifter covered in a vamp's dinner would only cause me more issues if another one of the bloodsuckers catches up with me. Better to bolt and hope no one does.

In the back of my mind, setting off another Claws and Fangs war is a definite possibility. Our people have had a shaky truce for more than a hundred years now. Do I want to be the reason that goes to shit?

At that point, I might as well walk into one of the annual pack meets myself with a big, flashing neon sign over my head saying "alpha here" with an arrow down pointing at me for those who haven't already figured it out.

Yeah. That's gonna be a no for me.

I've been hiding in plain sight the whole time I've lived in Muncie. Aleks's charmed fang kept me off the radar of the city's top predators, and Roman's blessing allowed me to coexist in peace regardless of me being a shifter or not. He hasn't revoked it yet, not even after Aleks up and disappeared, and I don't want to give the leader of the Cadre any reason to do so now.

I just hope that the Cadre's patrollers are too busy walking the perimeter, keeping Muncie safe from any prospective threats—while also trying not to look too closely at how I feel about the biggest "threat" being the nearby presence of Ryker's pack—to notice a lone wolf shifter tearing her way downtown, covered in a few lucky bites and more blood than I can explain away with an impish smile and a sassy attitude.

I get lucky. I don't run across another soul as I head back to my apartment, and by the time I'm racing around the back, dashing up the fire escape (since using the elevator in my state is a no-go when all of my neighbors are vamps themselves), I'm starting to feel a little relieved.

Phew. I just about made it home.

Nineteen flights of rickety, steel stairs later, I let myself into the apartment, taking a deep breath as I do.

It's habit. Can't help it.

My stomach twinges, and not only because the tang of vampire blood clinging to me is enough to make the strongest shifter want to hurl. Because the apartment? It *only* smells of me and Ryker and vampire blood.

No Aleks.

Again.

I bump my hip against the balcony door, closing it behind me as I move into the living room with a little less pep in my step than there had been a few seconds ago.

Every time I leave the apartment, I hope that he'll be waiting for me when I return. For six weeks, I've gotten my hopes up only for them to be dashed as I approach the apartment. His scent has faded almost completely since he's been gone, but I hold out stubbornly until I walk inside and realize—*again*—that he still hasn't come back.

Part of me wants to go out there, hunt him down, and drag him home. Too bad I don't have any clue where he's disappeared off to. Based on my run-in with the vamp earlier, he's not just staying out of my hair like I initially tried to believe. He's totally abandoned Muncie and it's all my fault.

Ugh.

As I head straight for my bedroom, desperate for a shower, I let my thoughts turn to my phone.

I don't often carry the device around with me since it's definitely more of a human thing and, most of the time, I forget I'm supposed to act like a human. I really only use it to keep in touch with my job, my co-workers, and my parents all the way in Lakeview. Most shifters don't bother with human tech; it's just not how we're wired. Unless we're in separate packs, we can communicate far more effectively with a well-struck howl than with words over a phone.

Aleks has been a vampire for more than two hundred years. In a lot of ways, he's still stuck in the past, and it's usually the same when it comes to his own device. Though he's the one who insisted I get one when I first arrived in Muncie and accepted his offer to move into his apartment, he rarely uses his, either. Mainly to keep in touch with Roman, since he's a trusted member of the Cadre and had a nightly patrol until he left, but I could always reach him if I needed to.

Earlier this afternoon, I forgot to grab my phone before I left for Charlie's. I had left it in the middle of my bed, and there it is. Even though I want nothing more than a hot shower and a couple of hours to put tonight behind me, I snatch it, hoping that maybe there will be another message from Aleks.

Every week he makes sure to tell me that he'll be back before I know it. I only heard from him three days ago, so it's probably too soon to hear from him again.

Still, with the adrenaline from my fight rushing through me, and the weight of Ryker's fang even heavier now that I'm alone in the apartment without him, I swipe my phone open and, with a quick jab, pull up the lopsided conversation I've been having with Aleks since he left.

I bite down on my bottom lip. I swear, I can taste Ryker there. It only goes to remind me just how much I love him, and how much I missed him while he was in the middle of the country for the latest Alpha meet.

But that's the thing, isn't it? He's not the only one I wished would come back. And as happy as I am that Ryker did, that he made it a priority to see me first, to be with me, I don't think I'll get over my lingering guilt and regrets until I can finally make the whole thing right with my roommate.

Maybe then, when Ryker accuses me of sticking around Muncie because of Aleks, it won't be a lie when I tell him no.

Before I lose my nerve, I quickly type out two words—**miss you**—and send the text to Aleks. It's an oversimplification of how I feel, but for now? It'll have to do.

Once I can't take the message back, I toss the phone back on the bed and, stripping as I go, slog the rest of the way toward my bathroom.

Shower. A little breakfast. Some more sleep.

Oh, yeah.

Sounds good to me.

5

Things are so different nowadays. Even compared to six weeks ago, it seems like my whole world's been turned upside down.

Case in point: my job slinging whiskeys and tending the bar at Charlie's.

When I first started there over a year ago, I took the job because I needed to make enough money to pay my own way. As grateful as I was that the vamp stranger who saved me from being dinner my first night in town had offered me a room of my own in his apartment, my suspicious nature didn't trust that he had completely honorable intentions.

Aleks tried to convince me otherwise—one of the first things he did was snap off both fangs so that I felt like I had nothing to fear from him—but I held firm regardless. I wouldn't accept his charity and if he really wanted me to stay with him, I'd pay. Rent. Food. Utilities. We'd be strictly roommates, that was all.

Of course, I discovered a couple of months down the line that his intentions weren't anywhere close to being "honorable". From the moment he first laid eyes on me, he decided that I was destined to be his mate for some reason. And, yeah, I probably should've realized that when he made a big deal of saying "mine" to fend off the Nightmare Trio who had been sizing me up for chow.

I didn't, though. Not even a little.

I blame Aleks for that. At first, he tried to explain it as just his claiming me because I was a shifter who would be, well, destroyed by the vampires in the city if I didn't accept his help. Naive Gem totally fell for that shit. I blame Aleks, but I guess I also have to blame how much I rely on my ability to know when someone's lying to me since I foolishly accepted that Aleks was telling the truth when I couldn't sense any deception coming from him.

And he was—for the most part. Without him interceding on my behalf, first with the three female vamps, then with his boss, Roman, they would've put me down just for being a shifter.

But while Ryker is a soft touch with an obvious "white knight" complex, he didn't save me out of the kindness of his heart.

Nope. He did it because his heart said I was meant

to be his, and even if the Luna made me the fated mate to Ryker Wolfson, Aleks held out hope that, one day, I'd return his feelings and choose him to be my bonded mate instead.

Then, after a year of hiding out from the fated mate I was convinced rejected me, Ryker showed up in Muncie and Aleks's plans for the two of us came out. A jealous Ryker threw in my face that the fang Aleks gave me within days of our meeting was the vamp way of marking me as his.

Then, when I confronted him, Aleks didn't even try to deny it. That worked against him and his intentions. Knowing that my roommate lied to me for so long had me turning to Ryker to make sense of my feelings while effectively wedging a gap in the friendship I had with Aleks.

Eventually, I made him take his fang back. Aleks blamed Ryker for that as well as the way I turned against him, while Ryker hated Aleks's guts for daring to try to claim *his* mate.

And then there's the little matter of their fight...

Two months later, and I'm still having to deal with the consequences of *that* incident.

It happened at Charlie's. Through a perfect storm of Gem fuck-up's, all of the precautions Aleks put into place to keep me hidden from my fated mate fell through at the same time, leading to Ryker tracking me down one evening when I was behind the bar.

As if it couldn't have gotten any worse, Aleks was also visiting Charlie's that night. He walked in on Ryker trying to explain to me that he hadn't stayed away from me so long on purpose, that I'd basically been M.I.A. for the whole last year.

Tensions were already high; at the time, seeing Ryker again was the last thing I had ever wanted. Aleks knew that—and my overprotective vamp goaded Ryker into a fight that he then threw on purpose.

Of course, I didn't know that back then. I just watched in horror as Ryker attacked Aleks viciously, tearing his chest wide open with his claws while Aleks was unable to fight back. He didn't kill the vampire, mainly because I finally managed to put a stop to the slaughter, though his loss of complete control—a rarity for Ryker—meant that he had a supe battle in front of plenty of stunned human witnesses.

Talk about a disaster. Not only did I have to give Aleks six bags of blood to patch him up, but I had to deal with the fall-out of unaware humans discovering that a male can have his chest be turned into ground beef and still be up and walking around a half an hour later.

In Muncie, not everyone knows that supernaturals exist. A good chunk of the population does—and Charlie's was a majority supe bar even before the fight —but it took a lot of explaining and a shit ton of lying to cover up the brawl from those who had no idea.

Unfortunately, the end result of Ryker coming down to Charlie's to claim me in the first place was my secret getting out; not that I'm an alpha, but that I was a lone shifter hiding out among the vampires. Basically, the supe population in the Fang City has finally figured out that Gem behind the bar wasn't as human as she appeared to be, and now they like to come down and gawk.

On the plus side, unlike the vamp who confronted me last night, most of Charlie's patrons don't really care that I'm a shifter so long as I keep their glasses topped off. Sure, I get my fair share of dog jokes—one downside of living amongst bloodsuckers, I figure— but they're harmless for the most part, just like my customers.

But that's for the most part. Halfway through my next shift, later on the same day as when I left Ryker's townhouse and fought that pervy vamp, the door to Charlie's opens, and in walk two vampires who are definitely *not* harmless.

The strikingly handsome male with the styled blond hair and pale skin is Dominic Le Croix, almost as high up in the Cadre as Aleks is.

In a way, I'm not surprised to see him walking into Charlie's. After what happened this morning, I was expecting some kind of reprimand from the Cadre sooner or later. Sue me for hoping it would be later, though.

But the redhead walking in beside him? I know who she is, too. That's Tamera, and seeing her makes me wonder if I'm getting more than a reprimand.

Wonderful.

I look past the pair, double-checking that I'm not missing something. This, uh, isn't a duo I expected to see walking into Charlie's together, and the serious expressions on their supernaturally stunning faces—not to mention the wide berth the other patrons give them—confirms that this isn't some kind of social call. Especially since that's Tamera who's with Dominic.

It's just... Dominic, I know a little bit better. He's a member of the Cadre, one of the sunset spotters. He patrols the perimeter of the city toward the end of the daylight, he's a close friend of Aleks's, and while he works directly for Roman, I've met him before—for a drink at that apartment with Aleks, or during one of our visits to Mea Culpa, the vamp night club—when it had nothing to do with his ranking as a powerful Muncie vamp.

But Tamera? While I've run into Gretchen from time to time on her own, any time I've seen Tamera, she's with Leigh. The three of them make up the fangy clique I named the Nightmare Trio, but from some of the gossip I picked up from a few of my vamp customers when they indulge too much, Tamera and Leigh are more than Gretchen's followers. They're a bonded pair who hang out with Gretchen in the hopes that the blonde vampire will become their third.

I had no idea that Tamera was a part of the Cadre 'cause no way is she here on a date with Dominic.

Play it cool, Gem, I tell myself. You got this.

As they approach the bar, I don't even pretend not to notice them, though I do step away to the far end of the long counter since it's obvious that they're here for me. The second they entered the bar, Tamera's head swung my way. Her scarlet nail followed as she pointed at me. A sense of self-preservation warns me that I'm probably going to want to keep this conversation as private as I can, so I move away from few customers who were enjoying their five o'clock drink.

I nod at them, grabbing a rag and wiping down this side of the bar. "Welcome to Charlie's. Can I get you guys anything?"

It's a kindness, a test, and me just doing my job all rolled into one. If they're on duty, alcohol is out, but they're both vamps. Charlie keeps the back fridge stocked with blood bags—both the real stuff and synthetic—so I could serve them something if they're thirsty.

Please ask for a blood whiskey, I think. Just a shot so I know that I'm not in as much trouble as I'm willing to bet I am.

Tamera's pale green eyes glance up at Dominic. Like every other vamp in Muncie, his eyes are just as light; blue instead of green, but so pale that they kind of freak me out. I fix my gaze on a point just over his shoulder so that he can't tell.

When around an apex predator, never show any weakness, even when they're wrapped up in such a respectable and lovely package.

Dominic glances down at Tamera, then shakes his head. "Nothing for us, but thanks for offering, Ms. Swann."

Oof. Ms. Swann.

I toss the rag while biting back a sigh.

Yup. I'm in big, big trouble.

Might as well just go for it, then. "Let me guess. This is about the prick from this morning, isn't it?"

Tamera is supernaturally beautiful—because, well, *vamp*—but her beauty fades a little when she twists her face into a sneer like that one. "If you're referring to how you attacked Monroe—"

"Tamera," Dominic says chidingly. "The Cadre doesn't judge until we have all the facts. We have Monroe's statement that a feral wolf attacked him. Does she look feral to you?"

A begrudging, "No."

"I agree. So now we're here to ask Ms. Swann for her side of the story. Can you listen with an open mind, or would you rather return to headquarters while I handle this for Roman?"

"I'll listen."

"Good." He waits a moment for her to say anything else, then offers me a small grin when she doesn't. "Roman believes in fairness, even if some of his people don't understand why. Still, Tamera's a quick learner and will be an asset to the Cadre now that she's joined us. I'm glad she's here to help with this evening's mediation."

As Tamera preens next to him, I can help but think: oh, he's *good*.

Instead of scolding her and making her feel bad, he corrects her behavior and lifts her up. I've seen Aleks do something similar, especially when he was talking to some of the vamps he worked with.

Roman's influence? Maybe.

I've never met the leader of Muncie, but I'm grateful for him all the same for all of the allowances he's made for me ever since Aleks vouches for me last year. Gotta admit, after how I lost my temper earlier, a part of me was almost sure that he'd kick my sorry tail out of Muncie once word got back to him about me attacking one of his people.

He could very easily still do that, but at least he's giving me the chance to defend myself first.

So I do. From the way Tamera's expression turns skeptical as I give a play-by-play of what happened between me and that Monroe asshole, I'm not so sure I pull off being as straightforward as I want to—my animal nature gets the best of me, emotions taking over as I remember what he said to set me off—but she doesn't interrupt. Neither does Dominic.

When I'm finally done, he nods. "Thank you. Monroe has a history of going after those weaker than him, then complaining when he finds one stronger. You're not the first. I'll bring your response to Roman, and maybe you'll be the last."

Whoa. I thought the way I just about tore him apart was payment enough for his challenging me. Luna, if I wanted the vamp taken out, I could've done it myself and saved us all the trouble.

Brutal.

I must have given away something in my expression because Dominic is quick to correct my suspicions.

"Please. We're not monsters, Ms. Swann. We won't kill him for going against our leader's wishes. If anything, Roman will just... encourage him to leave Muncie if he won't abide by our rules."

Because he seems to be siding with me, I make myself ignore his cheap shot. Oh, the benevolent vampires would never take down one of their own, would they? Not like the beastly shifters, huh?

Fine.

"Gotcha." I give him the "okay" sign, even though I'd really rather flip him the bird. "Well, thanks for coming down here. I should be getting back to work—"

Tamera taps the other vampire's arm. "Don't forget, Dominic. You also wanted to ask the wolf about the lamppost."

Luna *damn* it.

Think *innocent*, Gem, I tell myself. I stand by fighting Monroe—he totally deserved the ass-kicking I gave him—but the lamppost...

"Lamppost," I echo. "What lamppost?"

Dominic's lips twitch. I have no idea if vampires can tell when a shifter is lying the same way an alpha can, but he knows I'm completely full of shit anyway. I'd put money on it.

To my surprise, though, he goes along with it. "A few blocks down from here. There was an... incident last night. One of the posts toppled over and fell into the middle of the main road. You wouldn't happen to know anything about that, would you?"

"Uh..."

I swear, nearly all supernaturals act like they're so much better than humans because of their gifts, but after meeting quite a few of them this past year, I'd argue that humans have a couple of knacks of their own. Take my fellow bartender, Hailey, for example. The chick can't be on time to save her life, but, somehow, she has the perfect timing even so.

Like right now.

As soon as Dominic finishes asking me about the lamppost I kicked over earlier this morning, the door to Charlie's swings open, a frantic Hailey racing toward the bar. She's already wearing her Charlie's t-shirt, keys in one hand, a white envelope in the other, and her purse hanging off of her shoulder.

She runs right behind the counter, throwing her keys in her purse, snagging the strap, and tossing the whole thing onto one of the empty shelves beneath the bar.

"Hey, Gem. Sorry I'm late—" Hailey stops short when she realizes that I'm facing off against a pair of vampires who are still waiting for me to admit to the destruction of Muncie property. "Oops. Didn't see you were busy."

Busy, my ass. One glimpse and she knows that these two aren't any customers of ours. At least, not tonight.

Hailey's a human, but she's also a fang banger. Growing up in Muncie, she learned the truth about the supernatural world when she was a teenager and has made it her life's ambition to snag an immortal vampire mate of her own one day.

Hmm...

"I'm not busy," I tell her. True since, the way I see it, I'm done with this chat. "In fact, I was just finishing up with these two. But if they need anything else, I'm sure you'll be more than happy to help them." I smile at Tamera, ignoring the way her pale eyes bleed to red as I pointedly dismiss her, then gesture at Dominic's broad chest. "Hailey, have you met Dominic? He's Cadre, just like Aleks."

Hailey's eyes light up. She might be a non-supe, but I was right. She can pick up on a vamp from almost a mile away.

"I haven't had the pleasure," she says, her voice dropping to a purr. "Where's your glass, Dominic? Didn't Gem tell you? In Charlie's, the Cadre drink for free."

"When they're not on duty, that is," I add.

Hailey kicks my heel. She telegraphed her move so I could have avoided it, but I don't. I owe her one hit for basically cock-blocking her, but that point right there is a pretty big one. Roman would have the head of any of his people who drank while they're on the clock for him, and even though I know Dominic would refuse anyway, I have to remind Hailey that there are rules when it comes to playing around with a more powerful vamp like this one.

"Unfortunately, that is true," he agrees, "but I'll have to remember that for when I'm available." With a small smile for Hailey, I notice that his eyes are glued to her neck. I'm not even a little bit surprised that, when I turn my head just enough to get a peek, I see a barely clotted-over bite. Freaking Hailey. "And you're here often?"

"Most nights." She crosses her arms, positioning them underneath her boobs, giving her girls a bonus lift. Don't know why she bothers since Dominic's fixation is purely on the bite mark already left on her throat. She might know a vamp when she sees one, but he doesn't seem to mind that she's a fang banger at all. "If I'm not here, I'm usually at home. I live just around the corner. Not too far."

Now, I don't mean to stare at her chest. In that pose she's holding, her boobs are... well, they're *right there*— and that's when I notice that the envelope dangling loosely from her grip has one single name scrawled across it.

Gemma.

My name.

Wait— *what*?

Forget about Tamera and Dominic. Yeah, yeah, they passed along Roman's warning about tearing into his vamps even when they're the ones doing the provoking, and if they had any proof that I'm responsible for breaking that lamppost, they would've offered it up by now.

As far as I'm concerned, we're totally done here. They need to go because I'm suddenly curious to know why Hailey's carrying around an envelope with my name written on it.

Snatching it out of her grip would be rude, even for an alpha shifter, so I settle on calling her name.

"Hailey?"

It's like she can't hear me.

"Hailey!"

Still no answer.

What the—

It takes me another three times calling her name before she finally rips her gaze from Dominic.

"Yeah, Gem? What's up?"

"What have you got there?"

"Huh? Oh. You mean this?" She flashes the envelope at me but, for some reason, doesn't hand it over. "Jimmy gave it to me last week. He said a young girl with black hair gave him this envelope outside the bar, making him promise he'd give it to you. But you were off that night, so he gave it to me. I took it home, forgot about it, then only remembered to grab it earlier since I knew you were in today."

Okay. Not the sort of answer I was expecting, but now I'm even more curious.

I'm just about to ask for it when Dominic snares Hailey's attention again.

At least, this time, it's to say goodbye.

The smooth vampire reaches over the bar, holding out his alabaster hand to Hailey. She quickly switches the envelope from her right hand to her left hand so that she can take him. From my spot a few steps away from her, I can see Dominic as he runs his long, slender fingers over her pulse point.

He smiles, the points of his fangs peeking out over the edge of his bottom lip. "I'll be seeing you soon."

Hailey giggles while Tamera rolls her eyes.

Honestly, I'm kinda on her side with this one.

It takes a few more seconds before he finally lets go of my co-worker. With a stern look in my direction—okay, maybe I rolled my eyes a little, too—he wordlessly tells me that the Cadre has their eyes on me, then strolls out of Charlie's with Tamera at his side.

I don't think Hailey freaking blinks until the door opens, then closes behind the pair of vampires.

Just in case, I snap my fingers.

6

She jerks, like she's been ripped out of a trance.

Then again, considering I don't know the extent of a vampire's power or how they snare their human prey, for all I know, she *could've* been.

My brow furrows as both me and my wolf check her over. "Hailey. You okay?"

"More than okay," she breathes out. Not so sure about that. Her eyes are kinda dazed-looking, but she blinks again and starts to act a little more coherent. A little more like her normal self, too, especially since she seems starstruck after meeting the male vamp.

She just goes to prove I'm right by asking, "Who *was* that?"

"Dominic Le Croix. Cadre," I remind her. She must've missed the earlier introduction because she was too busy drooling. Whatever. I'm not too concerned since I'm pretty sure they're going to get to know each other better after what I just witnessed anyway. "Now, about that envelope—"

"Do you think he's interested in me?"

A human with an obvious vampire bite? I can't promise that he'll fall in love with her and make her his blooded mate, but I'm betting the powerful vamp knows an easy mark when he sees one. At the very least, he'll sample her blood.

"Yes," I tell her, my words ringing with honesty. "I do."

With her free hand, she reaches up, fluffing her hair. "He's gorgeous."

Yes, yes. Vampires are gorgeous. We all know that.

Before she can continue to gush some more, I jerk my chin at her other hand. You know. The one holding an envelope with my name scrawled on it.

"You said that was for me," I tell her.

Hailey glances down at her hand as if she'd totally forgotten she was carrying it. She blinks, then winces. "Sorry, Gem. Something about a sexy vamp makes me lose my head."

A sexy vamp. Blood loss from her, ahem, "date" with another vampire earlier tonight. Six of one, half a dozen of the other, if you ask me.

Whoops. There goes the eye-rolling again. It's an epidemic.

Reaching below the bar, I grab one of Charlie's

trusty charmed patches. There's magic in these vamp-designed bandages. Not only do they heal up a blood donor quick as anything, but they erase any bites as well as providing the nutrients a donor needs to replace their plasma. By tomorrow night, Hailey will be ready if Dominic decides to have a little nibble.

"Here," I say, holding it out to her. "Trade you."

"Thanks, babe."

While Hailey busies herself with activating the patch and slapping it over the marks in her throat, I try my best to make it not so obvious that I'm sniffing the envelope she handed me. I don't recognize the heavy hand that's printed the five letters of my name in the middle of the envelope, so I'm hoping I can get a hint about who it's from by scenting it.

Hmm. I get Hailey, obviously. Jimmy, too. And... a third scent that I don't recognize. Probably the chick who passed it along to Jimmy. It's certainly human, though.

I run my thumb over a nickel-sized bulge sticking out near the bottom. Whatever is jutting against the paper is hard. Sharp. It's a weird shape with no give to it.

I assumed the envelope was some kind of letter. It made sense, but now I'm second-guessing that assumption. The back of the envelope is licked, too, as if whoever stuck something inside of it didn't want it to fall out.

Welp. I won't know what's in there unless I open it so, ripping the envelope along the nearest corner, that's what I do. I stick my pointer finger inside, widening the hole, then shake the envelope so that whatever is inside drops out into my cupped palm.

I suck in a sharp breath when I recognize what it is.

A ruby.

No.

Well, yes. There's no denying it. It's cut, faceted, and probably worth a ton considering it's the size of a large pebble, and, yeah, maybe it could be... I don't know, like a garnet or a carnelian... but I know better. The shiny, red rock is a fucking ruby.

And it's not some kind of thoughtful gift.

It's a *warning*.

Oblivious to how I'm only a few seconds away from chucking the thing as far away from me as I can get it, Hailey looks over at the rock in my hand, goggling at it. "Whoa... that's a beauty. From your wolf?"

"Uh. No. I don't think so."

There are so many reasons it can't be from Ryker. He already gave me a necklace and after my less than enthusiastic reception, I can't imagine he'd try to one-up Aleks with this red ruby. Besides, it smells *human*. Of Jimmy, Hailey, and someone else. Someone I don't know.

Definitely not a wolf.

But, more than that, Ryker wouldn't have to play

postman to give me a gift. Now that we're firmly in the middle of our mating dance, his wolf would never trust anyone but Ryker to bring it to me. Like the necklace I'm still wearing. He'd need to see my reaction and watch me use it, just like he insisted on me putting the chain on right after he gave it to me early this morning.

That's not the only reason, either...

Hailey's lips pursed. "Your vamp?" she suggests. "Maybe Aleks sent it for you."

No. Not Aleks.

I shake my head.

For a moment, she looks stumped. But then she nudges me in the side. "Lucky bitch. Looks like you've got a secret admirer." She points at the ruby. "From the size of that thing, I'm thinking he's loaded, too."

If only.

Though my inner wolf is suddenly whining deep inside of me, I purposely pull a pleased expression. Happy, Gem. You're happy that some unknown person has given you such a pretty ruby that has no sinister meaning after all.

Uh huh.

Sure.

"Hey, Hailey?"

"Yeah?"

"I'm just gonna run and put this in the back. Don't want to drop this before I can even get a chance to say thanks to whoever got it for me."

My human co-worker is an open book. I can already tell she's about to push that exact topic, as if she's dying to know who'd give me an expensive hunk of rock like this in a simple white envelope after trusting it to strangers.

She's dying to know.

I wish I *didn't.*

Hailey opens her mouth again. It's gonna be another question. I'm freaking sure of it.

I don't wait around to hear it. Assuming she doesn't mind that I need a few seconds to myself, I spin on my heel, loping toward the backroom door with enough speed that, even if she hadn't already discovered I wasn't a human like she was, she'd probably guess.

Ryker wouldn't give me a ruby—because he doesn't know that I would see a rock like this and think it was something other than a pretty gemstone.

He doesn't know. He doesn't know that Gemma Swann is just a name my panicked mom picked specifically for me when we were on the run from my psycho sperm donor. She wanted to hide me and—as she put it—give me a second chance at a future where I didn't have to be Jack Walker's daughter.

Gemma was her second choice for my name when she was pregnant. Swann because it was the most gentle, non-threatening name she could think of in the spur of the moment.

But that's not my birth name.

I glare accusingly at the red stone nestled in my palm.

Ruby. Before I was Gemma, my name was Ruby.

And there are only a handful of shifters in the whole damn world who know that.

Me. My mom. My dad.

And... Jack Walker.

Shit.

Shitshitshit.

I exhale roughly, pacing around the backroom as my head spins wildly in thought.

So he *does* know. My bio-dad. As I squeeze my fingers around the gemstone in my grip, I have to accept that it wasn't a lucky guess after all. When Shane said that there were rumors that the Lakeview Pack was harboring a female alpha, that Wicked Wolf Walker was looking for a strong wolf to tame his wayward daughter, I was hoping that he wasn't sure. That he was guessing.

My name's different. For twenty-five years, I've been Gemma Swann, the adopted daughter of Paul Booker and Janelle Walker. As far as anyone knew otherwise, the pup that my bio-dad had with my mom drowned during my mom's escape from his brutal, abusive clutches. After that, she found an abandoned omega pup who definitely *wasn't* the daughter she lost, and she raised her with my adopted dad's love and support.

Ruby Walker doesn't exist. Only Gemma Swann does.

And that bastard is toying with me, letting me know that *he* knows that we're one and the same.

Fucking *wonderful.*

———

ONE UPSIDE TO PULLING TWO DOUBLES BACK TO BACK? Charlie doesn't mind when I call him up and ask if I can cut out a couple of hours early.

There's coverage. Our schedule isn't set in stone, either, so as long as I don't leave Tony and Hailey and Sherm short-handed, Charlie gives me the okay to cash out and go. And if Hailey suspects that my "generous" gift has anything to do with my early night, my human friend is too busy wondering when she'll see Dominic Le Croix again to say anything when I tell her that I'm done for the night.

I made it until eight before I couldn't take it any longer. From Hailey, I know that Jimmy was given the envelope last week; coincidentally, it was the day Ryker left for the Alpha gathering, and if it had gotten to me earlier, I would've spent the whole time he was gone freaking out alone.

A week is too long to even think about tracking down the chick with black hair. Apart from the basic description Jimmy gave to Hailey, I have no way to know who else is involved or how to find her. Wicked Wolf Walker is a no-brainer, but at least I can be reasonably sure that my sperm donor didn't march into Muncie to drop off a ruby in order to screw with me.

Oh, no. That's not his style. But relying on someone weaker to pass the message along? Even if they're human? That totally is, especially since Muncie is so well protected, it would probably take a human to cross into the city and deliver that damn envelope before Roman's patrol would let another wolf in.

Even so, my first instinct is to go searching for the mysterious black-haired woman. It's impossible, I know that, but my second instinct scares me so badly that I almost want to hunt Muncie for a ghost rather than give in to that other urge.

I don't, though. Instead, I reach into my back pocket and, my heart rate quickening, I take out my phone.

Under contacts, I have all of seven names. Three co-workers, Charlie, Aleks, my mom, and—

"Hello?"

At the rich, gravelly, familiar voice, I shudder out a breath. It scared the shit out of me that, with the ruby shoved in my front pocket, the one person I wanted to talk to most was Ryker. Not because he's an alpha. Not because I want him to protect me. But because I just wanted *him*.

"Hey. It's me."

"Gemma? What's wrong?"

Because something has to be wrong, right? Otherwise, I wouldn't actually be calling him.

Shifters don't really use phones. Ryker is no exception. As the Alpha of his pack, if someone wants to get in touch with him, they can arrange to talk with him in his office of a den inside of the Alpha's cabin. Outside shifters? They have to request permission to meet with him, and tradition dictates that it be done in person to show the appropriate levels of respect.

However, when he first started to seriously pursue me two months ago, he realized that I had a phone to keep in touch with my new human friends—and Aleks. Hell if he wasn't going to make it easy for me to reach out to him when he was in Accalia and I was in Muncie.

Of course, he'd rather I visit him up on the mountains. Since that's not happening anytime soon, he makes time to run down and see me. Calling on the phone is a last resort for him.

Me, too, I guess.

His surprise that I'm actually contacting him has my whole body tensing up. I don't know what that says about our... whatever we have. Relationship? I'll go with relationship. Because calling us 'fuck buddies' is just wrong in so many respects.

It's my fault. I know it is. Whether I can bring

myself to believe him or not, Ryker has made it clear that he's ready to be my bonded mate the moment I'll accept him. I'm the one who can't bring herself to take that plunge.

If physically mating is all we do, that's because I've made it that way by putting off actually *becoming* his mate.

I almost lie. I know from experience that my innate lie-detecting ability relies on my nose and I figure it's the same for Ryker. Over the phone, he'd never know I was lying—but I can't do it. I called him for a reason, and though I'm not really sure what that reason is, I find myself telling him all about the envelope.

It doesn't matter that the ruby is seemingly meaningless to him. I tell him that—to me—it's proof that the Wicked Wolf knows exactly where I am and how to get something to me, and that's all he needs to hear.

"I'm coming back. I'm leaving Accalia right now."

"What? No. It's fine. I'm... I'm okay. He dropped the envelope off a week ago—"

"Right," Ryker points out. "When I was in the middle of bumfuck nowhere with the other Alphas. He wanted you to be spooked when I wasn't around. Don't tell me that wasn't on purpose."

I can't. I already figured out the same thing, but that doesn't mean I need Ryker dropping whatever he was doing to, I don't know, hold my hand or something. I'm a big girl. I *was* spooked, but now I'm aware that my psycho sperm donor has eyes on me. He can use a human to get close to my job. I'll be more vigilant now that I know.

"Ryker. It's okay. I promise. I didn't call because I want you to protect me—"

"You're my mate." His snarl is so loud, I have to pull the phone away from my ear. "Like hell I don't. It's my job to protect you."

I know Ryker. Telling him that I'm not his mate—not officially—will bring that bulging vein of his out. Telling him that I'm a freaking alpha in my own right and he's wasting his time trying to stand in front of me might just make poor Duke explode.

I cling to the last thing he said instead. "That's not your job. Your job is to be the Alpha of the Mountainside Pack. You were gone for almost a week, Ryker. Don't drop what you're doing to come down here. I promise you. I'm fine. Besides, I'm heading home right now."

Translation: I'm going to the apartment, not your townhouse. Ryker could try to push me, but we both know that I'm stubborn enough to leave him out on the balcony if he insists on rushing down into Muncie anyway.

He's not giving up without a fight, the stubborn alpha.

"The pack survived the week without me. Anything they need from me can wait until tomorrow."

I gentle my voice. Ryker's wolf is evident in the edge of his tone, and if I don't calm him, he'll shift and run down the mountain even though I told him not to.

"Come tomorrow," I say instead. "Take the night to be with your pack."

"Gemma—"

I swallow, then force out, "Please, Ryker."

He huffs. "Fine. But I'm telling you, I'd much rather spend the night with you."

How does Ryker do that? With one frustrated yet completely honest murmur out of this male, I forget all about the threat of my father, the menacing ruby, the infallibility of the Fang City's constant patrols. Maybe I'd grown complacent, so sure that the Cadre's security would keep any other shifters out, but I can shove that all behind me when Ryker opens himself up to me like that.

Of course, then I think about how we left things earlier today. He swore we would finish the conversation I walked away from, but now that I called him, showing him some of my vulnerability, he's good enough to drop it.

He is.

I *can't*.

"About this morning..."

Ryker's reaction is the opposite of what I expect when I change the subject the way I just did. Instead of being angry again, he actually chuckles. The warm sound rushes right through me, sending a flash of heat all the way down to my toes. "What part of this morning? When I took you up against the wall?"

Ah, Luna. I glance around. Supes have amazing hearing, and while I didn't give a crap if anyone on the street overheard what I was telling him before, this... this is private.

My cheeks are already heating up as I remember vividly what it was like to have Ryker's big body caged around me. "Uh. I was actually referring to what happened after that."

"Oh. You mean when I bent you over the bed and made you scream my name."

"Ryker!"

Another chuckle. "Sorry, sweetheart. Can you blame me for wanting to remember the good stuff? I'd rather do that than have to think about you leaving me."

Oof. That one hurts a bit. I doubt that's what he intended by his blunt honesty, but still. I rub the heel of my hand against my chest as if that'll soothe the sudden sting.

"I'm sorry," I blurt out. "I shouldn't have done that."

He goes quiet.

"Ryker?" I look at my phone, checking to see if the call is still connected. "You there?"

"Yeah. I'm here. I just... don't apologize. I pushed. You pushed back. I should've expected it. You're an alpha. You acted like an alpha. I'm the one who couldn't take the challenge."

"There's no challenge," I tell him. I mean it, too. Maybe we'll never see eye to eye, and the two of us being alphas means that we'll probably always butt heads, but the challenges ended when I decided to see how the two of us could work together. "I might not always be able to tell you what I'm thinking or what I'm feeling... it might not come out right or at all... but there's no more challenges. I promise you that."

"Hey, you called me about the envelope just now," he reminds me. "It's a start."

It is, isn't it?

Huh.

7

R yker's not the only person I call on my way home—and while the conversation with him ended far better than it began, I wish I could say the same thing for the one I have with my mother.

I knew that he wouldn't understand why the ruby is so important, but my mom started getting upset the second I told her about it being sealed inside of an envelope with my adopted name on it.

Like me, her mind immediately jumps to Jack Walker.

"But how?" There's a crackling coming from her end of the line. Knowing my mom, she probably has me on speakerphone while she paces around Dad's den. "He's not supposed to know about you."

That's an understatement.

I've heard the story about how my mom finally had enough and escaped her abusive mate a hundred times over the years. Mainly from my dad, who always treated me as a fellow alpha. While my mom has spent my whole life trying to protect me from the reality of my birth father, my adopted dad knew I was strong enough to know the truth.

For three years, my mom dealt with Wicked Wolf Walker's cruelty, his infidelity, and his twisted urge to kill anyone who wrongs him. He holds the record for surviving the most Alpha challenges since, as my dad told me, the Wicked Wolf of the West considers every freaking thing a challenge. Even now, he rules the Wolf District with an iron paw, and it was the same when me and my mom lived there with him.

Up until I was about one-year-old, my mom managed to convince my bio-dad and the Western Pack that I was an omega, just like her. She covered me with her aura, using it to make me seem like one. But, eventually, my alpha nature was too powerful for her to shield and her mate discovered the truth: that I was an alpha female. Threatening my life—telling my mom that he'd drown me if she didn't bond with him and start cranking out as many pups as possible to make more alphas—was the final straw for her.

She escaped, and when the Wicked Wolf finally found her in Lakeview, she made him think I was dead. Drowned, she told him, just like his threat. I "drowned" in the river that separated the Wolf District from the old Lakeview territory.

He bought it. Mainly because he'd never guess that a weak, lowly omega could ever lie to his face, but also because he then challenged my dad to an Alpha challenge—the only one that he ever lost.

Sometimes I wish that my dad finished Wicked Wolf Walker off then and there. A good man, my dad let him live, but he always said that, if my bio-dad came after my mom again, he wouldn't hesitate to put him down for real.

The threat must've been an effective one since, twenty-five years later, my sperm donor has stayed to his ever-expanding territory, even after Mom and Dad moved their pack across the country to the East Coast.

With a whole country between us—and her ex-mate refusing to attend any Alpha gatherings that my dad might be at—my mom found it a little easier to believe that Jack Walker might actually forget that she was his fated mate. By then, she was mated to Paul Booker, her chosen mate, and she had her Gem.

But just because he couldn't try claiming her again after she bonded with my dad, Mom was still afraid. Her biggest fear was that her ex-mate would discover that I was alive. Even if he didn't, any shifter who learned my secret was a threat. Males would do anything to make a female alpha their bonded mate, even *force* me to be their forever.

Shane's proof of that.

Still, she never really figured out that, as a female alpha, I'm more than capable of protecting myself. Add that to the years of training my Alpha dad gave me, and I've never been worried about that.

Nope. *My* biggest worry was that my fated mate wouldn't want me.

Been there. Done that. Didn't matter that it was all one big misunderstanding. I still had to deal with Ryker rejecting me and my wolf.

I survived that, though, didn't I? And, squeezing the ruby in my fist as I swing around the back of my apartment building, I try to explain that to her.

Part of me wonders why I told my mom. Even if my dad's not sitting in the same room, listening to my call —and I doubt he is, since he's not butting in with some booming comments of his own—she's going to tell him. They're mates. That's what mates do.

For good reason, my dad hates Wicked Wolf Walker. Obviously. If it's tough to keep Ryker from rushing down here to watch my back, it'll be impossible to stop Paul Booker if he thinks my bio-dad is snooping around after all these years.

With Mom, there's always a compromise. Like how I agreed to monthly phone calls around the full moon to prove that I was fine, happy, healthy, and, oh yeah, not being bonded against my will, I tell her that I'll let her know the second there's any sign that my bio-dad's involved in terrorizing me.

After all, it could be Shane. I have to admit that. Shane, or any other of the Wicked Wolf's army of shifter goons. Just because he knows my name, that doesn't mean that he hasn't shared it with anyone else. Shane already admitted that he's working with the Alpha of the Western Pack. Now he's his Beta, so odds are he's involved.

I just... I just wish he wasn't. For Ryker's sake, I wish this could be some kind of prank that I'm too oblivious to make sense of.

I don't think it is. Neither does Ryker. And, after my discussion with my mom, I realize that I'm more rattled than I wanted to admit to even myself. Old Gem would've sucked it up, dealt with it on her own, and probably made plans to trade Muncie for some new territory.

Not this New Gem, though. Muncie is mine, just like Ryker is mine. No one is going to change that—not even a wannabe alpha.

However, before I can finish explaining that, my wolf yips loudly, catching my attention. I pause, senses immediately alert. As a shifter, my main senses—eyes, ears, nose—are constantly filtering information in so I know I'm not in any danger.

But something's still not right.

What is it, girl?

My wolf tilts her head back, snuffling through her snout. In my human form, I do the same, and—

Oh.

Oh.

"Mom?"

She was in the middle of saying something, but she immediately stops short before answering with a, "Yes, baby?"

"I'm going to have to call you back."

"One hour, Gemma. If I don't hear back from you in an hour, I'm calling your father. He'll send Max to make sure you're okay and you know you'll never hear the end of it."

Great. Max?

That's even worse of a threat.

At least Dad knows that I'm an alpha and I can take care of myself. My older cousin still thinks of me as a little girl, and an omega to boot.

"Okay. Sure. One hour." I shove the ruby in my front pocket, then grab the fire escape railing, taking the stairs two at a time. "Love you. Bye. Don't send Max!"

I end the call as I race up the stairs. My wolf is urging me to go faster, as if she's afraid that he'll be gone by the time I get up there, and no matter how we left things six weeks ago, my wolf's always been fond of my vampire friend.

When there's only one flight separating me from

our apartment on the twentieth floor, I pause, taking a moment to compose myself. The aura tickles at me; it's even stronger after my mad dash up the steel stairs. Swallowing back my sudden nerves, I jam my phone in my back pocket, then lope gracefully up the last few steps.

And there he is.

Aleks.

I can see him from where I emerged onto the balcony. The sliding door is transparent, and he's turned the light on so the whole living room is illuminated. As if he's waiting for me, he's perched on the edge of the couch, nose in a book like always.

A sound of pure amazement escapes me.

Finally.

He's home.

I KNEW I MISSED ALEKS—I EVEN SENT HIM A TEXT EARLY this morning saying exactly that—but I don't think I realized just how *much* I missed my friend until I see him sitting on the couch like I have a hundred times before. Those wire-rimmed glasses of his sliding down his nose, pale green eyes drawn to the page of his book. Always a physical copy, rarely tech, because despite living through the last couple of centuries, he's a product of his times.

As I stare at him from the other side of the glass balcony door, he reaches for the corner of the page before pausing. Slowly, he closes the book, setting it down on the coffee table in front of him.

Ah. He must've finally sensed me out here.

As a vamp, his senses are keen. For the year I lived with him, he always seemed to know when I was on my way back to the apartment. He'd have a cup of tea waiting for me nearly every time my end of shift coincided with him getting ready to go out on patrol. I thought it was because he was a vamp and could smell me despite his tea concoction covering up my shifter scent.

That would be a big, ol' nope. Aleks scented something all right—*himself*. The charmed fang he had me wearing around my neck made me smell more like him than anything else.

I don't have his fang anymore. Tucked beneath my Charlie's t-shirt, I'm wearing Ryker's canine fang. Not that I plan on telling him that.

After all, I just got him back after being gone for six weeks.

I push the door open, stepping inside.

"Gem?" He rises up from his seat, moving so that we're facing each other. "What's wrong? You look like you've seen a ghost."

It's his voice that does it. His cultured, softly

accented voice that draws me out of my shock at finding him sitting there as if he's never left.

"Really? I'd say it's more like you're the one who ghosted me."

Oof. Could I sound more accusatory if I tried?

It's not his fault that I couldn't give him what he wanted. Deep down, I know he blames me for not even giving him a chance, but Aleks doesn't understand what it's like to be a shifter. Vampires have their own version of a bonded mate, but it's... it's different than what exists between a mated pair of wolves.

From the moment I was a fifteen-year-old girl, I knew that I was meant for Ryker Wolfson, just like I knew that we'd eventually end up together.

Aleks's gaze flickers away, but not for long. He knows I'm a wolf, that prolonged eye contact is a challenge, but it's never felt like that with him before.

It... kind does now.

I tell my wolf to sit down and stop grumbling. I've got this. "It's been a while. Are you back for good now? Or are you just stopping in?"

A look of surprise flashes across his flawless features. Probably because he's not used to me speaking to him so coldly. That's a vampire thing—shifters run hot.

I missed him, and I don't blame him for going, except that's total shit. I *do* blame him. Six weeks? Six freaking weeks? Where did he go? What was he doing?

Why did he leave me?

I can't ask him any of that. I gave up the right to be anything but his roommate when I chose Ryker, but I thought he was my friend. That... that's what makes his abandoning me like that feel so personal. I thought we were friends, but I'm not so sure we ever were.

Especially when Aleks answers my demands with a cryptic comment of his own.

"I wouldn't have returned if it wasn't of utmost importance."

Utmost importance... suddenly, I'm thrown back to earlier today. To the visit from two members of the Cadre.

Great. Let me guess. While Dominic and Tamera were questioning me about my run-in with that other vamp, Roman was running to tell Aleks on me. And now that I've gotten into trouble with the Cadre, he finally decides to make a reappearance.

I should be grateful he cares enough, but I'm not. I'm just plain annoyed that he decided it was time to come home when he was ready to play my knight in shining armor again, just like he did the last time a trio of vampires were threatening me.

"Is this about Monroe?"

The outer rings of Aleks's pale green irises start to darken, a red-rimmed line bleeding in from the edge. "I heard what that lowly menace did to you. I was already on my way back when Roman passed along his apologies. I refused to accept them."

I blink. "He apologized to you?" When Aleks nods, my jaw drops a little. "What the hell for? I'm the one he was trying to bite."

"Evidently, he knows you once wore my fang. In vampire circles, that means I'm the one owed the apology. And yes," he adds, as I open my mouth to argue, "I know you returned it. That doesn't change anything. Unless another vampire marks you as theirs, I'll always have the stronger claim to you."

I never really looked too deeply into vamp traditions. I never thought I'd need to. In hindsight, that was a bad idea since Aleks was able to use my ignorance against me until Ryker filled me in on what all the seemingly innocent gestures really meant.

Like, oh, how wearing his fang around my throat meant that I accepted his pursuit of me.

I shake my head. Since continuing this line of discussion is a no-go for me, I have to change the subject.

"So you didn't come back because of Monroe. Was it the lamppost?"

Aleks frowns. "Lamppost?"

Oops. "Nothing. Utmost importance, huh? It had to be something to drag you back to Muncie after you were gone so long. Is it Cadre business?"

That would explain why he's being evasive on

purpose. Who knows? Maybe he left because of me, but stayed away because of Cadre reasons. Like how Ryker had to fly across the country for the Alpha gathering. Most Fang Cities are sanctuaries for vampires, each with its own ruling coalition. Maybe Roman gave Aleks an excuse to get out of town for a bit and I'm just being unusually self-absorbed by assuming everything has to do with me.

And then he has to go ahead and say, "Cadre business? You could say so. Any time someone breaches our borders, Roman must know about it."

Breaches our borders... Cadre patrollers only call it that when there's a shifter trying to get inside of Muncie. Vamps have an open invitation, and humans are free to come and go, but shifters aren't allowed in except for very rare occasions.

"Shifters?"

Aleks nods. "There's been rumors about wolves testing our borders. I've spent the last few weeks in Europe. Licking my wounded pride, I guess you could say. But as soon as I heard, I flew home. I arrived last week, but only made it back to Muncie this morning. Roman filled me in on everything. From your wolf sharing our territory to unfamiliar shifters trying to test our boundaries... I stayed away too long."

His remorse is obvious, from the way he runs his fingers through his curls to the way his shoulders slump.

But it's more than that, too.

"You're still looking out for me, Aleks. Aren't you?"

"Of course. I would never forgive myself if anything happened to you."

His words ring so true that I can't help what I do next. I relax just a fraction, stepping toward him. With a sigh, I decide to be honest with him, too.

"I missed you, Aleks. I hated that you were gone so long, and I'm so fucking glad you're back."

It's the truth. I missed him. I missed him so badly that, at night, when I didn't have Ryker to distract me, I would sense Aleks's empty room and feel an ache deep in my chest. He was the first best friend I ever had, and even if I never thought of him as a prospective mate, our friendship gave me the strong bond I thought I lost when I believed that Ryker had rejected me.

Luna damn it, I forgot about vampire speed.

Aleks is quick. Quicker than I've ever given him credit for. Or maybe I was too naive. I thought that I could tell him how I felt and he wouldn't twist it into something more.

But I guess I couldn't because he totally does. Before I can even react, he has his hands on my arms, pulling me close against his hard body. I can feel the chill of his skin against mine, and I shiver.

He leans down, but I purposely turn my head away.

His lips brush my cheek.

I jerk my shoulder, breaking free of his hold on that

side. Slipping my hands between us, I shove him. He's fucking lucky. If I used all of my shifter strength and he wasn't expecting it, I could've cracked his sternum. Instead, I just force him to take a couple of hurried steps back.

I resist the urge to wipe his kiss off of my cheek. It would be childish and rude, but what the hell? If I hadn't moved my head, it would've landed on my lips and I'm not sure even begging him would keep Ryker from going after Aleks if that happened and he found out.

"What are you doing?" I demand.

Aleks smiles at me. For a second, I'm even more ticked off that he thinks this is funny—but then I realize it's a sad smile.

"I had to check, Gem. That's all. I had to see if maybe... maybe, this time, you'd choose me."

"Aleks—"

He glances down at his arm. On his wrist, he wears this expensive gold wristwatch that is probably older than my dad. It's definitely an antique, in perfect condition, and I hate to think about how much it costs.

"It's almost nine. I promised Roman I'd meet him at his headquarters for a quick conversation before I take up my post."

Now, I know this is Aleks's attempt to change the subject, to smooth over that near-kiss. And, Luna help me, I let him.

"You're going back on patrol?" I ask.

He nods. "I'm back to stay. And whether my roommate wants me to protect her or not, I will because I have a duty to my people. I start patrolling again tonight, midnight to eight unless I find something. Otherwise, I'll be back in the morning if you need me."

Though there's something in his tone that has my wolf bristling, I choose to let that go, too. Instead, I focus on what he referred to me as.

Roommate, huh?

Well. At least we're still *something.*

8

The next afternoon, Ryker joins me halfway through my mid-day shift down at Charlie's.

I really expected him to show up last night. During our talk on the phone, he promised that he'd give me until tomorrow—the 'please' I tacked on to his name did miracles there—but as I tossed and turned, I couldn't stop thinking about how he said we still needed to talk.

He was right, too. We need to talk about so many different things. If we're gonna have any chance of making this work between us, I need to stop walking away from any serious conversations. And Ryker? He needs to stop making decisions for me that leave me feeling like I have no choice but to walk away.

I've also got to realize that, once I allowed him to court me without pushing back against him, I can't be a lone wolf any longer. If something affects me, it affects my intended mate, too.

Case in point: the envelope that Hailey handed over. The Wicked Wolf's not-so-subtle threat was geared right at me—the ruby made *that* obvious—but I've gotten a handle on Ryker's personality by now. Anyone who threatens me, threatens the Alpha of the Mountainside Pack, too.

Just like how any threat, no matter how tiny, to our relationship affects the both of us.

I waited until I sensed Aleks leaving the apartment before I threw my covers back and gave up on sleep. Things weren't even close to being settled between us, but Aleks insisted on telling Roman about the ruby. Like Ryker, he doesn't know why exactly my bio-dad would taunt me with that specific gemstone—when he guesses it's just because it *is* a *gem*stone, I don't correct him—but he's more concerned about the black-haired human who played delivery girl.

Roman would need to know, he assured me, and he still had to get to his patrol post on time. So, even though I barely got to see him, Aleks was gone in no time.

An hour or two later, when I shuffled out into the living room, I discovered that he left a cup of chamomile tea on the coffee table for me. It was cold, like it had been waiting for me for hours, but just seeing it there had a reluctant smile curving my lips. I didn't drink it—I could scent the added herbs that would cover up my shifter scent and, yeah, I think we're beyond that now—but it was such a small reminder of our old life together that I couldn't help the small grin.

He knew I'd have trouble sleeping. Thoughtful gesture if only I didn't read way too much into it. I mean, the chamomile itself was fine. But the herbs? Why not toss the charmed fang back at me if he really wanted to make it clear that he's trying to shield me again.

The worrying kept me up, but so did the guilt. I knew that Ryker would want to be told the second Aleks was back in the apartment, and I convinced myself that it would be inappropriate to run and snitch while my vampire roommate was in hearing distance. Then I realized that it wasn't snitching, it was respecting my partner, and I begrudgingly made the phone call.

Ryker had been no less surprised to hear from me at midnight than he was when it was eight o'clock. He took the news better than I expected, though, only offering to come down to see me one time. When I told him that Aleks had already left for the night, he accepted it, but I knew my overprotective, possessive alpha wouldn't be put off much longer.

So, yeah. When Ryker strolled into Charlie's around three in the afternoon, a dare written in every line of his ruggedly handsome face, I couldn't even be annoyed that he'd tracked me down at work.

He made a point to stake his claim by leaning over the counter, placing his hand to the back of my head, pulling me into him for a deep kiss. I had to grip the edge of my side of the bar top to keep my knees from buckling beneath me, panting softly when he finally broke the kiss.

Then, with a pleased smirk, he said, "Cleared my calendar for the whole rest of the day, sweetheart. Hope you don't mind the company."

I don't. Not even a little. Though my wolf curls up, cozy and content in the knowledge that her other half is just across the bar, I'm actually a little taken aback by how my human side gets a much needed boost having him near.

Charlie doesn't mind it when Ryker stops by the bar, either. Actually, I think my vamp boss *encourages* it. He stocks Ryker's beer of choice and refuses to accept a tab. Though he'll never come out and admit it, I think he's hoping that my unstable shifter mate will attack another one of his vamp customers. Since the fight between Ryker and Aleks, his supe customer base has gone through the roof, and it's become more of a haven for vamps and humans in the know if only because he can use the only two shifters in Muncie as a draw.

At first, I was resentful, but then I realized that Charlie's the best boss I could ask for. He lets me take care of shifter biz when I have to, he pays me a fair wage, and he doesn't micromanage. A win-win all around, especially now that he supports my relationship with Ryker.

Most vamps don't. Aleks has a reputation in Muncie and while a lot of my vamp customers—like Jane and Vincent, for example—teased me for being Aleks's claimed mate, they really thought I'd end up with him instead of a shifter. Of course, they thought I was human back then, but still. They're always going to side with one of their own.

Eh. I'm used to it.

Take this afternoon for example. Vin is a letch of a vampire, and though he constantly tried hitting on me before he knew about Ryker, it's slowed down some over the last few weeks. He still does it—but not when Ryker's hanging around the bar.

That should've been my first clue. About twenty minutes ago, Ryker suddenly stood up from his stool. He rapped his knuckles on the bar top, telling me, "I'll be right back," before he crossed the bar, then stepped outside.

It's the dinner rush. While Charlie's is a bar, we still serve a ton of apps and bar food—burgers, chicken sandwiches, bloody steaks—to those who want a little substance with their drinks. Natalie is serving while Sherm and me tend to the bar. I help out running plates when she needs me, and when I'm back at the bar, Vincent orders up another shot of chilled O-negative while telling me for the countless time that, when you take the dead in your bed, you'll always be fed, or some shit like that.

I don't know. I'm a bit distracted.

It isn't until I swat off another of his come-ons that I realize I shouldn't be dealing with this today. Ryker's here and it usually takes him baring his canine fangs just the once and Vin stares sullenly into his blood.

Huh. Ryker's been gone a while now, hasn't he? Tugging on my half of our bond, I can tell that he hasn't gone far. He's just outside of the bar, but he's been out there a lot longer than he should've been if everything's okay.

As soon as the busy rush starts to wind down, I snag Sherm by his beefy arm, telling him that I'm ready to cash out. It's six hours into my shift and I was planning on cutting out a little early since Ryker was in town. Sherm didn't mind so long as I hung out through the early dinner rush, so I quickly finish up, then head for the door to go in search of Ryker.

It's not like I think he's in trouble or anything. He can take care of himself, even as a shifter in a Fang City. But this... it's out of character for him. To tell me he'll be right back, then disappear for so long isn't like him. Something's up.

Right as I hit the front door, I peer through the glass and know immediately that I was right.

I freeze, my palm pressed against the door—but I don't push. I can't. I'm too busy staring at the scene in front of me.

I see Ryker. His shaggy, chocolate-colored hair is windswept, the color on his tanned cheeks high, almost like he's just finished a sprint. His jaw is tight, fists formed and pushing against his hips. Sweat has his black t-shirt clinging to his torso, outlining his muscular chest.

It's August. It's hot, sticky, and humid out there, and shifters already run at a higher temperature. But to look that sweaty and annoyed. He definitely just chased something down. He must've caught a hint of a scent, then went after it, bringing its owner back to Charlie's.

That's the only way I can explain the female standing a few feet away from my mate.

It's been two months since I last saw her—when she was boldly strolling into Ryker's Alpha cabin, just another set-up courtesy of Shane Loup—but apart from her looking a lot thinner and more tired than I'd ever noticed, she's exactly the same. From the big, bouncy, light brown curls to her dark hazel eyes and the sundresses that could've come out of Omega Gem's old closet, I'm looking at Trish Danvers.

And she's way, way too close to my mate.

I shove the door, just managing to temper my strength in time so that I don't shatter the glass;

Charlie would have my neck if I did. Then, my wolf pushing me to cross the space between me and my challenger, I burst out onto the sidewalk.

Ryker's head jerks toward me, but his closed-off expression gives nothing away.

That's fine. He's not the one I have questions for.

"You!"

Her senses aren't as heightened as Ryker's. That, or her sense of self-preservation just sucks. She doesn't know that I'm coming at her until I'm already close enough to strike her down.

A flash of fear crosses her pretty face when she finally does realize, but she stands firm. I'd respect that if it wasn't so obvious that she's expecting Ryker to protect her from me.

"What are you doing here?" No. *Wait.* "How did you get past the vamps that guard the perimeter?"

"I was just explaining that to the Alpha," Trish says. "When I crossed into this city, I told them that Ryker was really my mate and that I can prove it."

Only a lifetime of tamping down my wolf, of playing a part, of acting like Omega Gem keeps me from snarling and going for her throat. Plus, Ryker's shifted just enough that his body is between mine and hers. He's expecting me to go wolf on her and, yeah, he'll protect the weaker wolf if he has to.

It's what an alpha does.

Remembering that, I keep my distance. I figure six

feet is good enough, and if I lose control and lunge, Ryker should still have enough time to intercept me before I can reach her. He's quick enough.

I swallow, keeping my voice calm and steady as I ask, "And they believed it?"

"Luna, no. But it was worth a shot."

That, at least, makes sense. Of course the vamps in charge didn't buy her story. How could they? When Ryker met with Roman Zakharov to make sure it wouldn't start any kind of issues between his people and ours if he followed me around Muncie, he told the head vamp that *I* was his fated mate. He had his own proof—at the very least, the written agreement between Mountainside and Lakeview when the two packs arranged for me to go to Accalia to mate him after his Alpha Ceremony—so he couldn't be Trish's.

Honestly, I'm less concerned with how she got into Muncie than how she knew where me and Ryker were. As the only shifters allowed in the Fang City, the Cadre would know, but she would need to know to search Muncie first.

"Okay. Follow-up question. How did you even know to find us here?"

Trish bites the corner of her mouth. Her scent gives her away, as does her obvious nerves. Even before she says a word, I know it'll be a lie.

I guess I just wasn't expecting it to be such a whopper, though.

"I... I tracked you."

Come on, Trish. You can do better than that.

Seriously. She wants me to believe that, as both a delta and a banished wolf, she managed to cross into Muncie, not get caught by the patrol until she made her way to Cadre headquarters, and that she was then able to pick up mine and Ryker's scent all the way downtown when Roman's headquarters is at the northern part of the Fang City?

"You're lying," I say flatly.

Trish turns to Ryker. "Alpha—"

"Lie again and this discussion is over."

He doesn't need the added gravel and grit to his voice for the alpha command to take hold. Trish tucks her bouncy curls behind her ears, dropping her gaze so that she's staring at the sidewalk instead of at us.

"Fine," she snaps out. "It was the vampire, all right? He told me where to go if I wanted to try and convince the Alpha to let me go back home again."

The stink of her deception fades a little. Okay. A vampire's involved.

"Which one? Roman?"

Trish dares a peek up at me. "The scary blood-sucker? No way. I'm lucky he let me stay. I wasn't gonna push him for anything more than that."

So she did meet Roman. But if he wasn't the vampire who told her where to find us...

"Then who?"

"The same one who came and found me outside of River Run. The pretty one. You know. Your friend."

Ryker's eyes flash angrily. "*Filan.*"

"No. It's like Alex or something. He's got this dreamy accent."

"Aleksander Filan." Who I'm very quickly reconsidering whether he's my friend or not. Aleks told Trish where I worked?

Wait—

"What do you mean, the one who found you outside of River Run?"

River Run in the nearest shifter pack to Mountainside. About two hours away when we're in our wolf shape, I wouldn't think of them as our allies, but they're not our enemies, either. Ryker's pack stays on his territory, Kendall's pack stays on his, and there's no trouble.

Is that where Trish ran off to when Ryker banished her from Accalia? I don't know, I think I always assumed she'd tag along with Shane when he joined the Western Pack. But from everything we learned after his betrayal, it seemed less like Trish was working with Shane and more like he used her to try to better his own chances to become an alpha.

"I'm not like you, Gemma. I'm not made to be without a pack. If I couldn't go back to Mountainside, I thought River Run might accept me. But their Alpha could tell that my loyalty was back with my old pack and he put me on probation. I was still on it when that vamp showed up, telling me that he could arrange for me to apologize to you, too. That, maybe if I showed you that I really meant it, the Alpha might let me back into Accalia."

"Do you mean it?"

When she stays quiet, Ryker growls softly. Not enough to attract the attention of any passersby—supe or human—on the street, but more than enough to have the delta wolf trembling in place.

Ugh.

I don't want to feel sorry for her. I really, really don't. For almost a year and a half, I've loathed Trish Danvers for the way she pushed her way between me and Ryker. The snotty comments she made about me being an omega, the nasty looks, and the way she made me feel like I wasn't worthy of *her* Alpha.

Then she led me to believe that he was choosing her over me and I let my jealousy twist me into someone I didn't like being. For Luna's sake, I almost ripped Ryker's heart out of his chest. If I could've gotten my claws on Trish that night, that's probably the least I would've done, I was so close to being feral.

I'm not feral right now. The bond between Ryker and me keeps me grounded, so even though I still can't get over her nerve to stand here in front of Charlie's as if she has every right to intrude on my life in Muncie, I'm not angry, either.

Nope. I feel bad for her, and that's about all the emotion I can muster. She worked hard to be some kind of knock-off version of me to steal away Ryker, but it didn't work. She lost everything—and I have it all.

"I said," echoes Ryker, "*do you mean it.*"

Trish gulps, but she knows better than to refuse to answer him. "I do. I'm so sorry, Ryker. I... it's no excuse, but I thought I could make you happy. You're a strong alpha male. You would've eaten an omega wolf alive, and I didn't think you'd be able to get along with another alpha. I... I thought I'd be perfect for you. That you would be better off choosing *me.*"

"That wasn't your decision to make."

"No. It wasn't. And I regret it. I regret letting Shane get in my head, and I regret trying to tell you what to do. You were right to banish me from the pack, but I'm sorry. I'm so sorry. If there's anything I can do to get you to forgive me, I'll do it. I swear to the Luna, I will. Just... I want to go home."

Ryker crosses his arms over his chest. "Don't just ask me then." He jerks his chin in my direction. "You want forgiveness? Ask Gemma."

Oh, boy.

He's daring her. It's easy to see she regrets her actions, that she really means it when she apologizes to Ryker. But will she be able to show me the same remorse?

Trish shudders out a breath. For a second, I'm sure

she's going to refuse—and then she says softly, "Gemma. I... I made a mistake. A big one. I judged you when I shouldn't, and I made the cardinal shifter sin. I interfered between two mates. I regret it. More than regret it. I'm ashamed of myself. But I'm sorry. Nothing like that will ever happen again, I swear."

I shrug. "Okay."

They're both looking at me now.

What? Is this the part where I'm supposed to accept her apology or something? Because, sure, I feel bad for her, but I don't know if I'm a big enough person to shove everything she did behind me and get over it just like that because she said she was sorry.

"Gemma. Sweetheart. Can you come here with me for a second?"

I'll give Ryker some credit. The 'sweetheart' was a nice touch, but asking me instead of ordering me? If Trish didn't already realize that the relationship between us is like nothing she thought it would be, having the dominant alpha snapping at her one moment before asking me for my permission has to be like rubbing salt into her open wounds.

I nod, and Ryker tells Trish to stay put. Then, with his hand pressed casually to the small of my back, he steers me to the end of the block. If we keep our voices low, not even her shifter's hearing will be able to catch a hint of our conversation.

And that's if she'd even dare to eavesdrop in the first place.

"Okay," I say, purposely stepping away from Ryker's possessive hold now that we're alone. I can't really focus when he's touching me, but from the speculative look on his face, I can tell that I'm going to need my wits about me for this one. "What are you thinking?"

"I'm thinking I should let her come back."

Ugh. I was afraid of that. "Really?"

"I won't if you think it's better that I uphold the banishment. But the Danvers have been a part of Accalia for centuries. Her cousin is even on my pack council. Her family understood why I did what I did, but no one was happy to see her go. She apologized. It doesn't take an alpha to be that stubborn, but she bared her throat to us."

He's not wrong. I call vamps arrogant, but just like how Ryker gets itchy when I thank him, it's rare for a shifter—no matter their ranking—to apologize. To apologize is to accept that we were wrong. We'll never admit that if we can help it.

And she did.

Does that mean I like the idea of welcoming Trish with open arms? Luna, no. My wolf snaps her teeth at the idea that, while I'm down in Muncie, Trish will be living on the same mountains as Ryker. What if she has a convenient case of amnesia, forgets her apology, and makes a move on him again?

We're still not fully bonded. That's my fault, too. If we *were* bonded, my jealousy would be a non-issue. It would only be about strengthening the pack. With Mountainside's numbers dwindling, Ryker couldn't really afford to lose another packmate, especially one with such ties to the community. Plus, if he brings her back, it shows that he's the type of Alpha his pack deserves.

He's not a dictator, but a leader. And a good leader makes decisions that help their people, not hurt them.

I... I can't say no, can I?

As if he can tell where my thoughts have gone, Ryker lifts his hand, cupping my chin so that I can't look away from him. He's in total alpha mode. Despite being the same type of wolf, even I struggle to meet his gaze when he's like this.

Too bad he doesn't give me a choice. In this, we're partners, and he proves it by looking right into my eyes without letting his wolf overpower mine.

"Do you trust me?" he asks.

"Yes," I tell him honestly. "But I don't trust her."

He gives me a searching look.

If he pushes it, I'll let it go without another word. He's the Alpha, and this is a Mountainside issue. He chose to kick her out of the pack when he believed she was working against us, but if she's just as much a pawn in this as I was? He lost Shane. In order to stand against the much larger—and much more powerful—

Western Pack, we need as many packmates as we can get.

And if somewhere along the line I started to consider it *my* pack again, I'm just going to bulldoze right over that realization.

But he's not pushing it. He's actually waiting for me to help him make this decision together as a unit.

Yeah... that's another realization I'm not prepared for.

"I'm good with whatever you think," I tell him. "She was telling the truth when she apologized, and you know what they say: keep your friends close and your enemies closer." I smile to show him that I'm only a little bit serious when I call Trish Danvers an enemy. "Maybe it'll be better for all of us if she's back in Accalia."

Ryker strokes the underside of my chin with his fingers as he steps back. "If you decide she's not a fit for our pack, I'll banish her again."

"Good. I'll hold you to that."

That settled, we walk back over to where we left Trish. And while I expect Ryker to tell Trish that she has his permission to rejoin Mountainside, I admit I'm a little stunned when he says to her, "Come on. I'm taking you back to pack land."

And... that's where I draw the line.

I can't. Maybe, in time, I can find it in me to put my animosity toward this female behind me. Unfortunately, in the ten minutes or so since I discovered her outside of Charlie's, I still haven't managed to.

Good thing I told Sherm to hold down the fort. Tony's due in to take over at the bar in about an hour, and I think Hailey's coming back for tonight's evening rush. They don't need me right now which is good because I have something else to do.

"You mean, *we* are going to bring her back, right, Ryker?"

Ryker cocks his head in my direction. Trish, who radiated pure joy when Ryker gave her permission to go home again, deflates a little when she realizes what it is I just announced.

Yup. Good decision, Gem.

Before either of them can try to argue, I kick off my sneakers, then shift on the spot, shaking off the remnants of my work shirt and my black jeans. It's the first time I've gone wolf in two days, and though my wolf is eager to stretch, I glance down.

Phew. Just like Aleks's charmed fang, the golden canine that Ryker gave me transfers over when I shift forms. It had been almost an afterthought—I realized I was wearing it the second I gave my wolf the command to switch places with me—but I shouldn't have been worried. Ryker's a shifter himself. If he bought me jewelry that wouldn't survive the shift, it would've been his fault if it exploded like my clothes did.

Using my snout, I nudge my sneakers toward the

front door of the bar. Hopefully one of my vamp customers will recognize they're mine and save them for me. Clothes are shot, but those sneakers cost me sixty bucks. I might risk getting caught shifting in public, and I could've ruined Ryker's necklace by shifting so impulsively, but I wasn't about to ruin sixty-dollar work sneakers.

Oh, yeah. I totally know where my priorities are.

Then, cocking my wolf's head at them still standing there in their skin, I give them a look that says, "I'm ready when you are."

9

You would think that a run all the way up the mountains to Accalia, a pit stop to pass Trish into the hands of Audrey and Grant Carter, and waiting for Ryker to call a pack meet for his inner council before hightailing back to Muncie on my own would have given me time to cool off.

Yeah. Right.

It does the opposite actually. Especially during the long run back to the apartment, all I can do is obsess over everything that just happened.

I can't even blame Trish. Not really. Respecting her Alpha's wishes, she had been begrudgingly joining the River Run Pack—until Aleks talked her into crossing into Muncie, finding me and Ryker, and begging for a second chance.

Like, really? I thought that I didn't have anything

left to worry over after she left. Now she's back, and there's only one vamp I can blame for that.

Despite running for hours, I'm still fully energized as I lope down the backstreets of downtown Muncie. The way I'm feeling, I'm just about *praying* that the wrong vamp wants to start shit with me. Maybe then, if I take my frustration out on them, I might not want to go for Aleks's throat when I see him next.

No dice, though. As if they can sense the rage pouring off of my blonde wolf, no one—not a regular vamp, a human, or a member of the Cadre—gets in my way as I head around the back of the apartment.

I bound up the fire escape, throwing my wolf's shoulder into the balcony door to get inside.

One good thing for my shit mood: Aleks isn't in the living room.

He's not inside at all.

Did he pick up on my mood as I approached the apartment and high-tail it out of there? It would've been a lucky break for him if he had. I can't imagine where else he might be. It's barely after sunset, and I know he's not scheduled for patrol until midnight. Since his return, Roman gave him his old shift back: midnight to eight am, every day. It's not even eight o'clock at night yet.

Well, at least that gives me a minute or two to change. I'd been so angry when I burst into the apartment, I don't think I would've thought twice before shifting back to my skin to confront him.

Aleks *so* doesn't deserve to see me naked right now.

So I pad toward my bedroom, bristling as I go. As soon as I step into my personal space, I slam the door, then shift back to my human shape. My hair is a rat's nest, my bare skin covered in grass clippings and dots of mud.

Welp. I guess a shower is in order. I'll make it a cold one and hope that it does something to cool my temper.

Just as I'm finishing up, I hear the front door of the apartment open, then close. I can sense Aleks's vampire aura filling up the space so I know it's him out there; not like it can be anyone else since only a moron with a death wish would break into an apartment that belongs to a pair of supes.

I finish yanking my brush through my damp hair, tossing it on my bed before I storm across the room. I grip the doorknob, almost snapping it with how quickly I give it a turn, then shout out, "Aleksander Pietro Filan!"

Oh, yeah. I go full name with him over this one.

My door flings open and I stomp out into the hall.

"Yes, Gem?"

I'm still so stinking pissed at him for interfering with Trish that it's all I can do not to slash at him with my claws if only to let out some of the wild fury that's taken root.

I try to contain it. I'm not as feral as I was the night I first left Accalia, but this is a pretty close second. Because the first night? I was sure that Trish had successfully come between Ryker and me. Now? I know that she hasn't, but that's no thanks to this guy.

"Yes or no. That's all I want to hear from your mouth right now. Yes or no, Aleks: did you find Trish Danvers and convince her that she'd be better off begging for forgiveness from Ryker and living in Accalia again?"

"Gem—"

"Yes," I snap out through gritted teeth. "Or no."

His eyebrows wing up, but that's his only reaction other than a sigh. "Then, yes."

I knew that. Still, it hurts to have him admit it to my face like that. "You knew how she treated me. You knew how I felt about her. What she did, trying to make Ryker her mate when I was his intended. And you still went out of your way to invite her into *my* territory where she was able to talk to *my* mate without me knowing about it?"

"Gem—" he tries again.

I hold up my hand. "Save it. I don't want to hear your apologies."

His expression turns haughty. "I wasn't going to apologize."

He wasn't? "Are you serious?"

"Why? I'm not sorry."

"You should be."

"I know she was cruel to you, Gem. If I'm sorry for anything, it's that she saw you before I could tell you that I invited her into Muncie. But forgive me if I feel sorry *for* her. Like the little wolf, I, too, know what it's like to love someone who chooses another."

Little wolf. That's what he used to call me. Sure, he said mały wilku, but it translated as "little wolf".

Oh, great. Not only did he drag Trish back into my life, but he's also giving her the same name as me. Is he trying to hurt me on purpose? Or did I never realize that my vampire with his chilled skin had a cold fucking heart?

He's cold, but I'm burning up. I thought confronting him would help me handle my anger, but yeah. Totally wrong on *that* count.

Glaring up at him, the molten lava of my gaze meets the steel behind his pale eyes. For the first time since I've known him, I want to challenge Aleks.

I... I want to see him hurt, too.

His lips twitch just enough that I see his fangs lengthening.

This is the reaction that he's looking for out of me. Hell if I know why, but that settles it.

I can be a hothead, but I'm also super stubborn. He wants me pissed at him? Then I'm going to dial back my rage as far as I can. Tamp it down. Swallow it so that it festers in the pit of my stomach. Don't care. I'm just not gonna let him see it.

I grin. Aleks's smile falters.

Then, without another word, I spin on my heel and stalk toward my bedroom.

I make sure to slam the door extra hard, too.

FOR THE NEXT THREE DAYS, I STEW OVER MY ARGUMENT with Aleks.

It's easy, too. With the latest shake-up in Accalia, Ryker hasn't been able to leave the Alpha cabin, let alone take a midnight run down to Muncie.

I'm still pissed at Aleks, so I'm avoiding him. He wants to call me his roommate? Then, that's what I'll be. We might cross paths in the hall or in the kitchen, but I don't go out of my way to make our relationship like how it was before he escaped Muncie. For the most part, I stay locked in my room, except for when I'm at Charlie's or burning off some of my fury by shifting to my fur and letting my wolf tear through the park.

The full moon's approaching. Maybe if Aleks came back during any other phase, I wouldn't be holding such a grudge, but I can sense her approach like a loose strand of hair stuck beneath my shirt. It's annoying, I keep slapping at it, and I know that if I can just pluck it off my skin, I'll feel relief. But, like some of my thin, blonde hairs, the Luna is relentless and annoying.

Gotta admit, I'm probably being relentless and annoying, too.

When he realizes that he might've gone a step too far in making himself feel better, Aleks does try to apologize. Coming from a male who once told me that he could count the number of times he's ever apologized on one hand, I should've been honored to be the recipient of a second one.

At least, that's obviously what he thought.

Me? In as polite of terms as I could manage, I told him to shove his apology where the sun don't shine.

Tonight, I'm off from work. I spent the whole afternoon keeping myself busy with errands: grocery shopping, heading out to buy replacement jeans, even stopping to pick up take-out for dinner. Then, like I've been doing every night since Hailey gave me that envelope, I called my mom and talked to her and my dad for a little bit after I hid out in my bedroom.

Aleks doesn't have to leave for at least two more hours. I can sense him just down the hall. Call it petty as hell, but though I couldn't keep myself from picking up dinner for him, too—we often ate Chinese together —I pointedly told them not to include any sauce packets.

Ha. Enjoy eating your plain white rice without your added duck sauce, pal.

It's the little things, I think as I change from my clothes into a sleep shirt and shorts.

It's still early, barely past ten, but I'm ready to climb into bed. Following Aleks's lead, I've enjoyed borrowing a few of his finished paperbacks. I'm in the middle of a murder mystery, and without Aleks to talk to or Ryker to keep me... entertained, I decide to turn in and read until I'm ready to go to sleep.

I'm so busy trying to see if I can figure out who the killer is that I lose track of time. So engrossed in my book, when a blood-curdling wolf's howl rips through the night, so loud it reverberates against my closed window, I jump so high that I nearly fall out of my bed.

What the hell—

Scrambling out of my bed, I toss the paperback behind me as I race for the door. I throw it open, rushing out into the hall as I try to trace the echo of the howl.

Aleks is standing in the middle of the living room, glasses dangling from his grip. He must have moved out of his room while I was reading, and from the dark outfit he changed into—different from what I saw earlier—I'm guessing he was getting ready to leave.

Without his reading glasses, I can see that his pale green eyes have flared to a brilliant shade of red.

Yup. He's *pissed* pissed.

"What is your wolf thinking?"

"That wasn't Ryker." I have no idea who made that awful noise, and though I know instinctively that's a shifter, not a true wolf, I'm even more sure that it's not Ryker's howl. "It's a shifter, but it's not him. I'm going to go find out who it is, though. Maybe I know them."

Aleks blinks. It doesn't do anything to fade the angry red, but at least he doesn't argue with me. "You go. You'll handle this better than I would." He pulls his phone out of his pocket. "I'll get in touch with Roman. Let him know we have a breach."

"I'll be right back," I promise.

I'm kinda surprised that Aleks is letting me go on my own. As I run in my bare feet out of the balcony door, ignoring the way the pitted steel tears into my soles as I race toward the ground, I think about how most males would find an excuse to hold me back.

Another peace offering, I decide. An apology without the words.

Whatever. I'll take it.

As soon as my feet hit the sidewalk, another howl erupts into the night. I immediately turn toward the source of it. Unless I'm wrong, it's coming from the park.

Makes sense. In my experience, most shifters in Muncie end up gravitating toward the only stretch of greenery inside of its borders. Ryker did, before he had his townhouse. I did, as soon as Aleks's fang wasn't tamping down my shifter nature.

And now it's his turn.

Wolves in the wild communicate with howls. In my skin, I can't really translate what this guy is saying, but I know it's meant for me.

I'm right. Sometimes it's really a fucking curse to be right, like now. Because, when I track the source of that howl, I find a fully dressed Shane Loup leaning lazily up against a solid oak tree as if he's been waiting for me all his life.

Only my shock at coming face to face again with him for the first time in almost two months has me holding back.

Not my wolf.

She bares her teeth at him, ready to continue the fight we'd been in before four of his former packmates unwittingly got between us. She's sure she would've had him, and I'm thinking she's right about that, too.

"Gem. There you are. I was wondering if you'd answer my call."

Really? We're gonna have a quaint conversation like you didn't slash me across the face last time I saw you? Oh, and that was *after* you tried to convince me to dump Ryker and mate you instead?

I want to say that to him. I want to throw it in his smarmy, smirking face. But I can't. I'm too busy goggling at him.

What the fuck is he doing in Muncie?

"You shouldn't be here."

Not the most bad-ass opening line, but it's all I can manage right now.

Shane pushes off of the tree, taking a few steps closer to me. Smart wolf, there's still a good fifteen feet separating us, but he's still close enough to look me up and down, leering openly as he does.

"And you shouldn't be alive," he counters. "Did you know that you're supposed to be dead?"

"Did you know that, if I get my claws on you, you will be?"

My retort is nasty, but I punctuate it with a sweet smile. Anyone who knows me would take that as the warning that it is, but despite Shane thinking he *does*, he has no clue what the real Gemma is like. I have no problem using that against him if I can.

Shame he doesn't seem to be bothered by it.

"No, really, Gem. You see, my new Alpha told me a very interesting story. About how he lost his mate. He thought he lost his daughter, too. Drowned. Very ugly way to go. For twenty-odd years he mourned her, and then he discovered that maybe miracles do happen. That maybe she's alive. And here you are. What do you say about that?"

I say that he's full of shit.

Jack Walker bullied my mother. He hurt her. I'm almost positive he did worse things, too, but she's spent my whole life protecting me from the monster that was my sperm donor. She told me enough to make me understand he was dangerous, then kept her secrets after that.

As a rebellious teen, I pushed. My wolf wanted to protect her, my hormonal human side wanted revenge.

My *real* dad was the one to sit me down and set me straight. Wicked Wolf Walker was dangerous, he was cruel, and if he never discovered that I was his blood, then we'd all be better off.

I scoff over at him. "I don't know what kind of fairy tale your Alpha told you, but Paul Booker is my father. No one else, especially not some murderer."

"You tell yourself that. You were young when your mother stole you away from your father. You might not even remember him. You certainly don't know him. He's a good wolf, Gem. A good shifter. He deserves your respect."

He's pushing me on purpose. If he knows anything at all about Jack Walker, it's that every single word he just uttered is a lie—and, yet, I can sense that Shane believes it whole-heartedly.

Time for a little reality check.

"One hundred and fourteen."

"Excuse me?"

"That's how many Betas the Wicked Wolf has gone through since he's been Alpha. One fourteen. You prepared to be number one fifteen, Shane?"

"I'm not worried about that. Still, it's impressive that you know his history," Shane remarks. "Even down to the number of former Betas who failed him."

I shrug. "I keep tabs on my enemies."

Or, at least, my dad does.

Shane smiles. I'm sure he thinks it's a charming grin, especially when he makes his dimples pop like that. "What about me?"

"Depends," I shoot back. "You my enemy?"

"I'd rather not think so. I don't want to hurt you, Gem. Of all the things I plan to do with you, pain will only be involved if that's something you're into. But make no mistake: I'll do what I have to to get what I want."

Of course. Even though shifter tradition makes it clear that a mate gets to choose—*has* to choose—Shane's another stubborn, selfish male who thinks he can decide for me.

I should challenge him for his arrogance alone. I might still, too, but first I have to figure out how he managed to get this far into Muncie without any of the patrol stopping him.

"How did you get in here?"

So help me, if he's been working with Trish after all and me and Ryker fell for her sob story the other day—

"Everyone thinks that shifters and vampires are mortal enemies. And maybe we are. Luna knows these parasites make me sick, but they have their uses. But let's not waste time with that. I have to be heading back to the Wolf District to make my report to the Alpha, but I couldn't wait any longer."

"For what?"

"Did you like my gift?"

I narrow my gaze at him. On the one hand, I want to know more about the vampire helping him. On the other, the change of subject is so abrupt, he has me on guard.

"What gift?"

"Don't tell me that you didn't receive my envelope?" Shane tuts. "Never trust a human with a simple delivery. I knew I should've just dropped it off at your blood bar myself."

"*You* gave me the ruby?"

"A male can't court his mate without a gift."

Ugh. Pardon me while I gag.

If that's what he was trying to do, he can have that sucker back. My hand slaps at the front of my thigh, searching for the ruby in my pocket. Crap. These aren't my jeans. I ran outside in my pj's. The ruby is back at the apartment.

Still, I say, "You want it? I'll go get it for you right now."

"Nah. It's yours. I want you to keep it."

That settles it. It goes in the trash the first chance I get.

"Don't do me any favors, Shane. Besides, I already know who my mate is." Reaching under my shirt, I yank out the chain that Ryker gave me. "Newsflash, asshole. It's not you. It'll never be you. So, unless you want me to dig my claws in your gut and see what you ate for dinner, you'll back the fuck off. Muncie is my territory. You're not welcome."

It doesn't matter that I'm a chick. The level of my dominance compared to a beta's is off the charts. Knowing that I mean every word of my threat, Shane should be backing down.

But he isn't. And when he reaches beneath his own shirt, pulling out a necklace that is eerily similar to mine, I know exactly why he's so damn confident— and why he's walking around the Fang City like he's untouchable.

Because that? That's a vampire fang. Wearing one of those means that he's under the protection of one of the fanged supes.

In Muncie, that means he *is* untouchable.

10

"Where did you get that?" I demand.

He couldn't just steal it. It's part of the magic. If a vampire presented you with a fang, it stayed on the chain. If you wear one meant for someone else, the fang crumbles to ash within seconds of being outside of a vampire's mouth.

No. Someone gave him that.

Hey. Maybe, if I'm lucky, he unwittingly accepted some vamp's proposition to make Shane their mate. Then he could give up on his insane plan to take me as *his* so that I can help him become an alpha.

"Stefan. For the right price, he was willing to help me sneak in right under the useless patrol's nose. And with a little help from my new Alpha and his latest pet, I covered my scent so that you wouldn't know I was here until I wanted you to. By the way, you look cute with your hair braided. I liked it."

I wore my hair in a messy braid style yesterday morning.

Does he mean to be so freaking creepy? Because the idea that Shane's been stalking me for real, not like one of the games I treat as foreplay with Ryker... that's super freaking creepy.

Don't let him know he's gotten to you, Gem. He'll enjoy it, and you'll be at even more of a disadvantage.

This sucks. My fight with Monroe, that sucks harder. I'm beginning to wonder if that was just shit luck after all. If he could buy this Stefan guy off, how much do I want to bet that Shane sicced Monroe on me the other night? If he's been watching me as long as he wants me to think—considering the envelope initially made its way to Jimmy Fiorello more than a week and a half ago now—then maybe he found a way to put me at odds with the Cadre.

If I wasn't already on Roman's shit list for fighting Monroe out in the open like that, I might've risked pissing the Cadre off by challenging Shane while he wore a vamp fang in a Fang City.

I can't, though. The last thing I need is another visit from Dominic or Tamera.

Worse, what if it landed me an eviction notice from Muncie?

He'd like that, wouldn't he?

Well played, Shane. Well played.

"Anyway," he drawls, and I have to resist the urge to snarl over at him, "I just wanted to tell you. The ruby? It was your father's idea. I still want you to consider it a mating gift, but it's more than that."

"Oh, yeah? What is it?"

I didn't think his dimples could be that deep. But as Shane widens his smile, the tiny craters in his cheeks only become more noticeable.

"It's a summons," he tells me, almost gleefully. "The Alpha of the Western Pack is calling you home. And, believe me, I did my research. I know exactly what happened to every last one of those one hundred and fourteen Betas so that I don't end up one fifteen. If you ignore his summons? You'll *wish* he was as lenient with you, Gem."

And then, before I can come up with another retort, Shane Loup has the nerve to blow me a freaking kiss before he strolls back into the park, content in the knowledge that—right now—there ain't a single thing I can do to stop him.

Bastard.

To make matters worse, when I slink back to the apartment with my tail between my legs, Aleks isn't there.

Not like he should be. He has his patrol to worry about, and if he got in touch with Roman, odds are the leader of the Cadre called him over to headquarters. One of the main reasons why I've never met Roman is that he rarely leaves the penthouse that the Cadre is based out of. And, like most older vamps, he doesn't care for the telephone. He expects his reports in person so of course he'd order Aleks to HQ.

I try to tell myself that that's fine. I'm more pissed that Shane blunted my claws by walking into Muncie with a fang of his own than the fact that he was responsible for the ruby that had me obsessing these last few days. The summons from my dad? That's not even something for me to worry about. Unless he wants to march into Muncie and drag me out kicking and screaming, no way in hell am I going anywhere because Wicked Wolf Walker wants me to.

Still, this is a new complication that I don't freaking need.

It only takes a few minutes of debating with myself before I go searching for my phone. I'd left it behind on the charger which was probably not the smartest thing I could've done since I ran off toward the sound of the howl without knowing just *what* I was running into, but it hadn't occurred to me at the time. Now, though? I need it.

I'm just finishing my call when I sense Aleks back in the apartment. I quickly hang up, tossing the phone somewhere behind me as I listen. Soft footsteps echo down the hall before stopping just outside my bedroom door.

Knock, knock. It's such a gentle rapping sound. *Knock, knock, knock.*

I almost call out that the door is open, that he can come in, before I think better of it. Inviting Aleks into my bedroom? Yeah. Probably not the best idea.

"I'll be right there," I yell out instead.

Through the wood, I hear Aleks's accented voice say, "I'll be in the living room waiting for you."

Works for me.

I give it a few seconds, then leave the bedroom. My boots hit the wooden floor of the hall so much louder than his careful steps, I can't help but notice.

If he recognizes that I've changed out of my pajamas, he doesn't say anything about it. He just rises up from the couch, giving me a careful once-over as if making sure that I'm in one piece.

It's nowhere near the leer that Shane gave me while I was still in my pj's, but something about the worry in his gaze has me feeling just as uncomfortable.

I clear my throat. "I thought you went out on patrol."

"Not yet. I had to go see Roman." Yup. Thought so. "So you know, he is aware of the situation."

"Well, that howl was fucking loud. I think everyone in Muncie is aware of the situation."

"Not that. Stefan."

I didn't even get the chance to tell Aleks anything about who was out there, why they howled, or how they got into Muncie. I was just about to when he drops that bomb on me

"Wait. You know about Stefan?"

"Roman does," corrects Aleks. "He suspected that one of our kind was working with one of yours. There have been rumors of a vampire being paid hand-somely to do so, and that added to the border breaches had Roman on high alert. After the howl, he sent the patrol to search for the wolf. I'm sure you know why."

He's right. I *do* know. It wouldn't matter if a shifter has permission to living amongst the vampires. Roman insists that we keep our supernatural status under wraps. He might look the other way for some reckless shifting, but making the unaware humans believe wild wolves are loose in the city? Yeah. Not Shane's smartest idea.

"It was easy to track him to Stefan. The sunset spotter that let him in earlier recognized the fang. He's already been taken in, his fate decided." Aleks waits a beat. "Roman sentenced him to death for putting his greed over the safety of our community. By now, that fang your wolf wears will be ash. He won't be welcomed into Muncie again."

Wow. Looks like Dominic was a little wrong. When

it came to a threat to his people, Roman could deliver justice as swiftly as any Alpha.

That doesn't really bother me, though. If I could've gone after Shane earlier, if the fang hadn't protected him, I would've done the same thing.

No. I'm more worried about how easy it was for Shane to work with a vampire to get to me.

Shifter packs are insular communities. We live together, hunt together, even trade together. We intermingle with the rest of the world only when we have to. Because of their diet, vampires coexist with humans better than shifters do. But when it comes down to the rivalry between our two kinds of supes, we hate each other. I don't know the history of why we do, but ever since the last Claws and Fangs war two centuries ago, it's just been a fact.

Then again, I guess it doesn't matter who hates who. Money talks, right? Stefan sold his people out for a payday.

Well, that also explains how Shane made it through Muncie last time. Not to mention the wolf who I caught scent of outside of Charlie's all those weeks ago. I didn't recognize the scent, but if my bio-dad has found a way to make our noses useless, for all I know it was *him* who'd been watching me that night.

Great going, Gem. Because *that*'s a thought I want to have right now.

"That's one vamp, Aleks," I tell him. My words are

dull. Flat. I've lost most of my anger, the adrenaline leeching out, leaving me feeling utterly drained. "I found the wolf who paid off Stefan. He bragged about it, showed me the fang."

"So Roman's right. The other wolf came here for you, too."

I never got to explain to Aleks who Shane was or what he wanted with me; first, because Aleks had left, then because it didn't really have anything to do with him. It's a shifter thing, and I doubted he could understand why a beta wolf would go to such lengths to force me into a mating even after he admitted that he doesn't love me. His argument is that he doesn't *have* to love me. To get what he wants from me, he could be a loyal mate who might grow to love me in time.

Like, don't do me any favors, right?

Aleks wouldn't get it. If I told him about Shane, he'd automatically assume that he wanted to steal me away from Ryker because he's in love with me— because *Aleks* is.

Better to keep it in-pack than involve a vampire.

So, though it's not quite the truth, it's not exactly a lie when I tell him, "You could say that. He's really after Ryker, but I'm just a pawn in his plan."

Aleks huffs. "Of course it involves the Alpha, too. Let me guess: that still won't have you seeing that I would be the better choice for you, will it?"

I wince. Not because he landed a blow with his

words, or because I'd rather not hurt his feelings again, but because he said that right as Ryker appeared on the balcony. I can see my intended mate over his shoulder, and from the blank expression on his face, I know that Ryker was in time to hear Aleks's question.

When I don't answer, Aleks follows the direction of my gaze. He stares at Ryker just long enough to be rude without triggering a full-on Alpha challenge before turning back to face me.

"Gem? What is he doing here?"

I exhale roughly. "Shane's his former Beta. I had to tell him that he was howling in Muncie."

"I told you I would go to Roman and take care of it. Didn't you trust me?"

I look up at Aleks, over his shoulder at Ryker, then back to my vampire roommate. "I trust you," I make sure to tell him, "but you're right. I'll always choose Ryker. I called him because he needed to know, but I asked him to come see me because I needed him. I'm sorry."

Aleks nods. One single, solemn nod. "I understand. In that case, I'll leave you to him. If you don't want my protection, there's a whole city out there that does."

Ouch.

RYKER DOESN'T SAY A WORD UNTIL WE'RE OUT OF earshot of the apartment.

At first, I think it's because he's trying not to rub it in Aleks's face that I left with him, but it doesn't take long for me to realize that he could care less about that. In fact, if he wasn't already bristling with barely contained fury, he probably would've purposely done just that if only to remind Aleks to keep his fangs off of me.

When I spoke to him earlier, he seemed aggravated that Shane pulled another stunt and frustrated that the fang kept me from doing anything to run him off my claimed territory. He also acted a little skeptical when I asked him to bring me to the townhouse so we could be together, but he's not a fool.

My default is to tell him that I'm fine, that he doesn't need to rush down to babysit me. For me to basically plead with him to come over, he had to know that I was more rattled than I wanted to let on. Considering how fast he made it from Accalia to Muncie, he had to have run as a wolf most of the way, only stopping to grab a change of clothes before he bolted up the fire escape.

The bare feet give him away, too. Most shifters store a shirt and pants—in Ryker's case, they're cheap sweats and an undershirt—around places where they might not want to be caught naked. Shoes are usually optional.

They are for him tonight.

We agreed that I would wait for him at the apartment, but then we'd walk over to the townhouse together. I wasn't worried that Shane hung around after his howl, and after talking to Aleks, I'm sure he's gone. Walking with Ryker isn't about me being worried, but to prove to him that I'm not afraid to walk around Muncie at night—with or without him.

He's acting weird, though. He hasn't said a word, and when I moved to walk beside him, he fell back a step so that he was trailing behind me instead. I figure it's because he's guarding my back, but something's rubbing my fur the wrong way.

And then, while waiting to cross the next street, he says, "We can't do this anymore," and I swear to the Luna, my heart stops beating for a second.

I pretend to misunderstand. "Do what?"

"You. Me. *This.*"

What is going on here?

"Are you trying to break up with me?"

I meant it to come out as a joke. A flippant remark. Unfortunately, my old insecurities didn't get the memo because there's no hiding the pure worry underlining my question.

"What? No. You're my mate, Gemma. Nothing changes that."

If only that was true. I'm his fated mate. Maybe we

can push it and say that I'm his intended. But I'm not his *mate* mate. Not yet.

Something warns me against reminding him of that. Despite his assurance just now, I can't shake the feeling that he is trying to break our bond.

"Okay. You're not dumping me. So what the hell are you talking about?"

He gestures with his hand. "This," he says again. "You being here. Me being in Accalia. I had no idea you were in trouble until you fucking *called*, Gemma. Shane could've done anything to you and I wouldn't have been able to stop him."

Is that what he's worried about?

"Please. I can handle Shane."

His growl is a rumble deep in his chest. "That's not the point and you know it."

"Yeah?" I raise my eyebrows at him. "So what is the point?"

"Our bond's strong, but it's not complete. I can sense where you are all the time now, but unless you're next to me, I don't know what you're thinking. What you're feeling. That'll change when you finally accept me as your mate, but until then, you're in danger. And I'm not saying you can't take care of yourself. I know you can. You're strong. An alpha. But I'm an alpha, too. My wolf snaps at me to protect you all the damn time, but I can't do that if you're in trouble and I find out after it's over."

Oh.

Okay, then.

"Shane got to you," he continues, running his hand through his shaggy hair. With his wolf in control, his claws are out, leaving track marks through the thick strands as he shoves it out of his face. "This time, he was just fucking with you. What if he's better prepared next time? What if the Wicked Wolf decides to take offense to you ignoring his summons and comes to get you himself? How will I know?"

I hear in his outburst what he doesn't want to accuse me of: *how will I know if you don't tell me*? Because that's the thing. If I talked myself out of telling Ryker earlier, he'd never know unless Shane found a way to taunt him next.

"Is that what has you so worked up?" I ask him. "That our bond's not final and you can't use it to check up on me?"

"Gemma, that's not—"

I don't even wait to hear the rest of his denial. He might not think that that's what's bothering him, but it is.

Luckily, I have a solution.

"We can fix that pretty easily, you know."

Ryker goes still. Around me, the world keeps spinning, traffic keeps going, and we probably could've crossed the street twice already, but we stand on this corner together as if we're the only two people in the whole fucking world.

"What did you say?" he demands.

"What? Maybe it's time. The full moon is in four days. Let's do it. Let's do the Luna Ceremony and become bonded mates."

For two months, Ryker has been after me to say yes. He vowed he would get me to change my mind, that every single time I stubbornly told him that I'll never be his mate, I was only lying to myself. He was right, too. I've known all along that I'd choose him again. I just wanted to wait until the right moment.

Now seems good.

And then Ryker's jaw goes tight, his dark gold gaze turning almost black as he says one word: "No."

No?

No?

I freeze in place while my wolf throws her head back in an anguished howl.

11

It hurts to think I'm being rejected again. That I put myself out there, finally accepting Ryker, only to have him reject my offer to bond with him.

The old Gem would've lashed out. Not gonna lie. The new Gem kinda wants to do the same. But I've gotten to know Ryker Wolfson these last two months. This male would only reject me if he felt like he had a reason to.

Last time, I didn't wait around for an explanation. This time?

I'm expecting one.

"Explain. Please."

"It's simple, Gemma. I won't bond you to me just to piss off your mom's ex-mate."

Oh, come on. He can't possibly believe that? Kudos

on remembering not to refer to that piece of shit as my dad, but still.

"That's not what this is about—"

"It's not?"

"No."

The look Ryker gives me lets me know that *he* knows that I'm lying.

My frustrated breath comes out in a rush of hot air. "It's not! Look, I'm not gonna stand here and tell you that it won't make our lives easier. If we're bonded, Shane will have to stop with this crap. He wants to mate me so I can help him become an alpha. Fuck no. And I'm sure my sperm donor has a similar plan. We can bond and put a stop to it, but that's not the only reason why I'm saying yes now."

Ryker moves into me, another one of his blatant dares. "Then why are you?"

Because I love you.

I open my mouth. I try to force the words out.

I can't. Not until I hear him say them first.

"Yeah," he shoots back. "That's what I thought."

Okay. I've had one hell of a night. I had to listen to my mom worry that her psycho ex was gunning for me. Shane's howl scared the crap out of me, then I went and dealt with him. I had another awkward conversation with Aleks.

And now this?

I shove Ryker away from me. "Back off."

His eyes flash, suddenly turning molten as if I've tripped his switch of something. "Excuse me?"

"I said back off, Ryker. I can't do this. Not with you. Not now. Especially not so soon after my run-in with Shane."

My wolf wants blood. She's not picky about who she gets it from, either, and I don't want another situation where I go for Ryker's heart.

So, rather than stay on that corner with me, I turn and start to jog across the street.

He just about catches up to me in five strides.

"Where are you going, sweetheart? You running away from me again?"

Whirling on him, I jab my pointer finger into his chest. Only when I hear his thin shirt rip do I realize that my claws are out.

I hurriedly fist them so that I don't mark Ryker up again.

"Don't chase me." My words echo with an alpha's command. I doubt it'll do shit to Ryker, but my wolf needs to find her voice regardless. "I told you I'll go with you to the townhouse. I'm going. Just... let me walk there alone. I need some time to think."

For a moment, I think he's going to fight me on this. But he doesn't. Grabbing me by the chin, he holds my head steady long enough to give me a claiming kiss, then lets me go.

"If you're not at the townhouse when I get there,

the hunt's on."

My lips tingle from the force of the kiss. Even so, I force them into a rueful smile. "You'll never make it there before me."

It's another dare, and when Ryker's eyes seem to blaze in acceptance of the challenge, I wonder if that was my smartest move. He turns and sprints away, already looking to take a lead when I remember to shout after him, "Skin! Stay in your skin!"

The vamps already had to deal with one wolf tonight. Ryker got lucky that no one caught him running to the apartment earlier, but I don't want to take any other chances.

Then, when his bark of a laugh tells me that he'll still beat me while in his human shape, I take off in another direction.

One bonus to calling Muncie home? I know all the shortcuts. Ryker's long legs and incredible speed as a human might give him the advantage, but I know how to get to the townhouse quicker than he does. And, after I threw down that gauntlet, no way will I let him beat me there.

That's the plan. Too bad someone else has a different one for me.

Later, I'll accept that taking the shortcut through the abandoned part of the downtown area was my mistake.

There's a three-block radius that was the site of a

rogue vampire massacre nearly a hundred years ago, back when Muncie was a total Fang City, more vamps than humans. The previous leader of the Cadre tore through half the population of humans over the course of three nights, and a good chunk of the vampires who lived here.

All of his carnage was contained to the former site of the Cadre headquarters. After they caught him and destroyed him, the blood washed away, but the vampires considered it cursed. No one would willingly live near the site of the massacre. When more humans moved to town, the property still sat there vacant. Vincent, down at the bar, would tell stories about the screams he heard that night after he had a few blood-and-whiskeys, and he swore some nights, he still could hear them.

Normally, I avoid this part of Muncie because it gives me the freaking creeps. But, well, I had a race to win, and cutting through this part of the downtown would guarantee it.

Because it's abandoned, it's easy to sense when it's not. Though vampires don't register as alive to my wolf, I've gotten good at knowing when one of the undead is near thanks to their bloody scents and their icy auras. It's not usual for one of the fanged supes to hang around here, but I'm not too concerned when I realize that one's nearby.

The living being I pick up on? Yeah. That one has

me pausing for a second.

No scent. Unless they're approaching me from downwind—and they're not, I can tell—the imposing male figure has no scent. He's hiding it, but even if I can't figure out how he's pulling that off, it doesn't extend to *his* aura.

There's an alpha wolf out there—and it isn't Ryker.

I immediately drop to a defensive crouch, taking in my surroundings. Like most of the downtown area, the blocks are filled with tall buildings, shops squeezed alongside the skyscrapers, apartment buildings reaching up to the nearly full moon. They're all empty, though, their windows covered in dust, the stink of old, forgotten blood still clinging to the cement.

"Ruby…"

It's that name. That fucking name.

My head jerks toward the west.

Fitting.

There, about four blocks in the distance, I see a tall, imposing feature. He's just on the edge of my line of sight and, using the moon, I take in his features.

Holy shit. He looks like an older, male version of me.

The blond hair. The honey gold eyes. The delicate features that give him a set of movie star-handsome looks. A muscular build. A tailored suit.

A vicious smile.

The Wicked Wolf of the West.

At that moment, twenty-six years of anxiety, of fear, of *hatred* for my birth father come roaring to the surface. My wolf remembers him, remembers the things he used to do to my mother, remembers how he'd pick her up by the scruff, throw her against the wall, then laugh while my mother cried and my wolf whined.

She has no loyalty to Jack Walker. She wants to see him dead, and I'm happy to oblige.

I poise myself to shift, letting my wolf have the honor of taking up the challenge that bastard Alpha threw at my feet by coming into my territory and using that name from the past.

However, right before I do, the whisper of the vamp closing in on me is suddenly undeniable.

He's at my back. If I don't defend it, I'll never get the chance to go over to the Wicked Wolf.

Jumping to my feet, I turn on the vampire sneaking up on me. Good thing I reacted when I did since he's only about twenty feet away from me. If I'd hesitated any longer, he might've had me.

That pisses me off, but not as much as the grin of delight wrapping around his fangs.

Already knowing what I'm going to find, I spin around.

Fucking *damn it*. He's gone.

A distraction. He snuck his way into Muncie to distract me, and now I'm facing off against a vampire who already has his fangs fully extended, his pale eyes bleeding over to vivid red.

Glaring over at the vampire, I snap out, "I have bigger prey to go after. So turn around, walk away, and I'll spare you. 'Cause, trust me, you don't want to do this."

The vampire hisses at me. It takes me a second to realize that that was supposed to be a laugh. "Oh, believe me. I very much do want to do this."

Hang on... he doesn't have *two* fangs extended. He has *one*.

Great. How much do I want to bet that the other one is currently in the possession of Wicked Wolf Walker?

"Stefan wasn't the only one, was he?"

"He got sloppy tonight. I heard he got caught. I won't. And when I deliver you to your master, I'll have the money to take on Zakharov and the satisfaction that I've personally rid Muncie of a bitch in heat."

Dog cracks. Ha, ha. So funny.

Excuse me while I *don't* laugh.

"He didn't just get caught, dumbass. Roman executed him for betraying Muncie."

"You see? That's exactly why we can't let Zakharov be in charge any longer." Pointing at the sidewalk below his feet. "Marcel was a good leader. When he was the head of the Cadre, we ate like kings. None of this hiding from donors, working with mutts. Vamps ruled the whole city, and now we patrol for the vermin who crept in under the door. Not anymore."

Marcel. Marcel Claret. I know who that is. The rogue vampire who let the power go to his head and murdered hundreds.

Good going, Gem. As if me walking this way wasn't creepy enough, now I'm facing off against a vamp who's *proud* of a mass murderer. Not only that, but I'm in the middle of the streets where they once ran with the blood of his victims with no one around to hear *me* scream.

Except—

Oh, please. Please, please, please. Just this once, I'll give him a pass. For following behind me, for chasing after me, for going against what I asked him. If the tug on my bond can be trusted, I'm not alone, and if that's so, I'll never, ever bitch about Ryker's overprotective nature again.

Just then, the vampire pulls something out from beneath his dark jacket, and he has all of my attention.

The moon reflects off the blade, revealing that it's a knife. The sinking pit in my stomach when I see it tells me that it's a *silver* knife.

If he gets me in a vital organ with that sticker, I'm dead. No amount of regenerative properties will heal a fatal wound made with silver.

"He doesn't want you dead," the vampire tells me. I have no doubt in my mind who the 'he' he's referring to is. "You know I could kill you with this and no one would stop me. If I have to I will, but I'd rather you come quietly."

"How do I even know that's real silver," I call out, buying some time for Ryker to get here. "You could be bluffing."

Real smooth, Gem. I was trying to distract him, but I failed to remember how freaking quick a vamp can be. Within seconds, he's closed the gap between us, lashing out at me with the blade.

He wasn't trying to kill me. If he wanted to, I know he could've. The strike was just a warning, and he did it perfectly. With just the tip of the silver blade, he cuts through my shirt, digging into my side. Immediately, I bend over, gasping as a scream rips out of my throat.

My side feels like it's on fucking fire for seconds that, as I suffer, feel like *hours*.

He whirls around me, returning to his place. My eyes are glazed over in agony, so I only hear his taunts as he says, "There. Now you know I was telling the truth. Fight me, and I'll stab deeper the next time. Be a good little girl and—"

I never discovered what would happen if I was a good little girl. His words cut off just as I'm able to blink away some of the subsiding pain. It still hurts, but it's manageable, and I force myself to stand straight just in time to see Ryker attack the vamp from behind.

I want to shout out about the silver knife, but I

don't need to. Ryker already knows about the dangerous blade. The first thing he does is use his claws to slice through the tendons at the vamp's wrist. Blood sprays across the sidewalk, but he loses his grip on the knife.

Ryker uses the side of his foot to kick it out of the vamp's reach. He made sure it hit the handle, leaving him unharmed as he turns his attention on the vampire's killer fangs next.

The only way Ryker was able to disarm him so easily was because, this time, *I* was the distraction. The vamp was too cocky to realize that Ryker had snuck up behind him until it was too late. Of course, that doesn't mean he's going to lay down and make it easy for Ryker to fight him. Not like Aleks did. This vampire might be working with my dad, but it's obvious he despises shifters.

He wants to kill Ryker as much as my male wants to kill him. Ryker just wants it more, and he proves that by wrapping his hands around the vampire's throat. Before the vampire could snap his fangs and try to bite Ryker's hands off of him, Ryker uses all of his brute strength to pop the vamp's head off of his shoulders like he's a freaking dandelion.

Without a second thought, he throws the head as far away from us as he can, letting the vamp's body crumple to the sidewalk behind him. Then, his predator's gaze locked on me, he runs right over to where I'm standing, stunned at the quick yet brutal way the fight just ended.

"Are you okay?" His hands are running up and down my arms, leaving streaks of blood where he touches. "Where did he get you?"

"Just my side. Not deep enough to do anything but hurt like fucking hell so, yeah, I'm okay. I swear."

Ryker pulls me into his arms, squeezing me so tight I gasp out a breath. "I heard you scream. Damn it, Gemma, I didn't think I'd get to you in time."

"But you did," I point out, lowering my voice in a bid to help calm my riled-up alpha mate down. "You came back for me. You *saved* me."

"You're my mate. You've always been my mate. I'll never let anyone hurt you."

Like so many times before, when Ryker calls me 'his mate', I know he means it to the depths of his soul.

We could wait. I never want to go into a bonded mating for the wrong reasons. That's what I've been telling myself for *months*. But then he touches me and I forget all the reasons why I wanted to wait, why he agreed. Why I thought I was proving something—to him, to me, to the freaking Luna, for all I know—by refusing to tell him how much I love him.

Tomorrow's not promised. The dead vamp proves that. If I want him to know how I feel, there's only one way I can do that.

"I love you."

I don't need him to say it back, either. I just watched him rip a head off of a vamp with his bare hands for daring to slice me in the side with a silver blade. If that doesn't scream 'I love you' as a shifter, then I'm being thick on purpose.

He pulls back just enough to get a good look at me as his brow furrows in concern. "What did you say?"

That I love him. Why does he look so confused, too? It's not like this is the first time I've been honest and open and confessed my feelings to him. He should know that I love him by now, right?

And, okay. Professing my love to him when he's not in the middle of mating me is different from me doing it in the middle of the street, with two pieces of a vampire corpse turning to ash behind me.

My side twinges but not bad enough that it can keep me from rising up on my tiptoes so that we're eye to eye.

"Gemma—"

Cradling his stubbled jaw in my hands, I start peppering kisses all over his face. In between kisses, I pant out the three words over and over again. By the time I'm clinging to his neck, my forehead pressed to his hair, I don't want there to be any doubt about how I feel.

And then Ryker runs his big paws up and down my back. "You scared the shit out of me just now. What would I do if anything happened to you? I love you, too, sweetheart. So, so much. Don't ever do anything like that again."

I told myself just now that I didn't need the words. His gesture was enough. But hell if I don't squeeze him even tighter to hear him whisper them back to me, even if it came in between him scolding me.

My laugh is shaky at best as I let go of his face, giving him some space. "I was just taking a shortcut to get to you. I didn't expect an ambush."

"You're an alpha wolf, Gemma. You have to always be expecting an ambush."

I wish he wasn't telling the truth.

"Why? When I know I have someone I adore watching my back."

"I'll always watch it. I'll never let anything happen to you," he promises.

Luna, I hope he means that, because I can't stop myself from blurting out, "Then be my mate. Forever. For always. It's your turn, Ryker. Just... say *yes*."

I hold my breath, telling myself that if he refuses me again, it's not a rejection. Mates get to choose. When he was ready, I wasn't. If he's not ready now, then fine.

I can wait.

I—

"*Yes*."

I throw myself back into his arms, blood and gore and all.

12

The Luna Ceremony can only take place during the full moon. That's four days from now.

That doesn't mean that we don't go back to Ryker's and fuck like bunnies because, oh boy, do we. Pausing only to shower off the last of the vamp—and, okay, I might've jumped on Ryker's cock even while we were rinsing off—we immediately fall into bed together.

We're shifters. We fight and we fuck. That's what we do.

Ryker is still battling his protective urges. He tells me he saw his forever flashing before his eyes when the vampire went after me with the silver knife, and even if he knows that he's risking Roman's wrath by killing the vamp, nothing would've been able to stop him.

After I let him use my body to get through the worst of them, I collapse on my back before shoving him off of me. Ryker's still hard—surprise, surprise, right?—but he takes the hint, curling up against me while he gives me a second to breathe.

Unfortunately, the second to breathe turns into a second to obsess.

"Roman's gonna be majorly pissed that we killed that vamp," I announce to the ceiling.

"That parasite is pure alpha. He'll understand why we had to."

I've never met Roman, but everything I heard about him makes me think that Ryker's right. Or maybe he's just trying to make me feel better because I gave him a blowjob in the shower before I let him do whatever he wanted to me and, yeah, that put him in a much more generous mood.

"Mm."

That's all I can say. I don't want to disagree in case that riles up Ryker's wolf again, and I'm also a bit distracted myself as Ryker scoots down the bed, laying one of his massive paws on my naked belly as he brings his mouth closer to me.

I've come three times already tonight, but if he's willing—

Ryker laps at the cut in my side.

Oh.

I watch his head move slowly, nuzzling my skin as

he tends to the healing wound. Because it was from a silver blade, it's going to take longer to heal, but it will eventually. I won't even have a scar—at least, I won't until the night of the Luna Ceremony when I finally let Ryker mark me.

It's such a sweet gesture, I almost forgive him when he glances up at me and says, "Besides, it doesn't matter if he gives a shit or not. You have territory of your own where he can't threaten you."

And... here we go again.

Every time we mentioned possibly bonding to one another, I always made it clear that I might do it one day, but not if he expects me to drop everything and move back to Accalia.

I don't want to think of ours as a long-distance mating or anything, but more like an expansion of our territories. I could visit him in Accalia, he could come see me in Muncie, but I'd still live here, still work here.

I knew he wasn't happy, but that was my condition. One of them, at least, but the one I was going to stick to the most.

"You know I haven't changed my mind, right? Not about becoming your bonded mate, and not about staying in Muncie. I love you, Ryker, but I love my life here, too."

He lifts his chin, nipping his canines against the underside of my boob. "I know."

I jerk a little at the tiny jolt of pain before it hits me what it was that he said. "You know?"

"I want you as my mate. Together forever, Gemma. No matter what."

I want to believe that so badly.

"Even if I want to stay here? I'm not saying for forever, but for now?"

Another nip. But, as much as I love what he's doing to me, this conversation is important. I smack the top of his head gently, drawing his attention back to me instead of my boob.

He shrugs, running his hand lazily across my belly. "Sure. But only if I can stay with you."

That's the last thing I thought he was going to say.

"What? Ryker... you belong in Accalia."

"Correction." A swipe of his tongue beneath my boob. I let that one pass because it feels so fucking good. "I belong wherever you are."

"Of course, but—"

"No buts. I already bought this place."

And... another shocker. "What? *When*?"

"When you told me that you're the Alpha wolf of Muncie. This isn't my home, sweetheart. It's ours. Why do you think I've spent so long trying to get you to like it? To stay?"

I blink. I... I don't know what to say.

That's okay. Ryker isn't done yet.

"Downstairs can be the den. You can invite anyone

inside." He pauses, his molten gaze cooling slightly as he adds, "Within reason."

Translation: *not Filan*.

"But up here?" he adds, slowly pulling my legs apart so that he can climb between them, his lips already lowering to my pussy. "This is just for us. Okay?"

"I—"

He uses his nose the nuzzle my clit before taking it in his mouth, sucking it gently.

"*Okay.*"

———

I STAY THE NIGHT.

Way I see it, if I'm going to take over the townhouse, I should get used to it, right?

The next morning, Ryker returns to Mountainside to make arrangements. I almost offer to go with him, but I have things I have to take care of myself. With the full moon being three days away, it's going to be tough to arrange everything. I've got to cover my shifts at Charlie's, pack everything I need for an extended stay —Ryker insists on at least a week for just the two of us after the night of the Luna Ceremony—and... Aleks. Yeah. I've got to do something about him.

We decide that we'll meet up at the townhouse tomorrow night and drive into Accalia together. That gives me today and tomorrow to get everything in order, then one more night together until it's time for the full moon.

Call me a coward, but I've got my claws crossed when I finally head back to the apartment to pack up the afternoon I'm supposed to leave. I couldn't bring myself to go the day before, and I blamed it on the vamp that attacked me. If I see Aleks, I'll have to tell him, it'll get back to Roman, and... I wasn't ready for that yet.

I'm also a freaking liar. Sure, I'm worried about Roman, but my biggest concern? Facing Aleks and telling him that I'm bonding myself to Ryker in a couple of nights.

So I didn't.

Instead, I finished my last scheduled shift at Charlie's, then returned to the townhouse where I tossed and turned all night in an empty bed.

I have to tell him. It'll be even more fucked up if I get mated and he has no idea. And I know I'll have to face Aleks sooner or later, but that doesn't stop me from letting out a monstrous sigh of relief when I arrive at the apartment and he's not home.

I'll still have to talk to him, though, so before I lose the nerve, I pick up my phone.

I ignore the two missed calls from my mom, reminding myself that I'll have to call her later. There's also a call from Hailey, plus a text that says she's seeing

Dominic for dinner tomorrow. I think to myself, "More like she'll *be* his dinner", and, snorting under my breath, I pull up Aleks's name.

There's a long paragraph from him. I read it with a pounding heart, exhaling softly when I get to the bottom of it. Roman knows about the vamp attack—Ryker decided it would be best to contact him yesterday morning to explain what happened—and the Cadre leader decided an execution was warranted. Not only are we not in trouble, but Ryker got a personal thank you from Roman which, even through text, I can tell pissed Aleks off.

Then, before I think better of it, I shoot off a text of my own to him.

Meet me at seven. The place where we met. We need to talk.

By the time I'm packed and ready, it'll be close to the time I agreed to meet Ryker, but I have to take a couple of minutes to see Aleks. After all he's done for me this last year, it's the least I can do.

I shove my phone in my back pocket and try to forget about it. I know him. He might not answer my text, but he'll be there because I asked him to.

And then I'll tell him.

It's not goodbye. I'm coming back. Maybe not to the apartment, now that Ryker wants me to move into the townhouse with him, but I don't have to make up my mind about that yet. For now, it's just a small vacation.

That's what I tell myself as I grab a handful of panties, stuffing them into one of the three open suitcases I've pulled onto my bed.

A vacation.

I'm not moving out yet. I'm definitely not going back to Accalia to stay.

And if I tell myself that enough, maybe I'll believe it.

—————

At promptly seven, I drive my Jeep to the edge of Muncie territory. A solitary figure is standing is waiting for me, staring up at the mountains in the distance.

Aleks.

Two Junes ago, I fled Accalia in this very Jeep. It was packed with everything I owned, not just three suitcases, and I planned on driving until I could forget the sting of Ryker's rejection.

Fate had different plans for me, though. I'd barely gone from pack land to vampire territory when the Nightmare Trio—Gretchen, Leigh, and Tamera—stepped out from the shadows, ready to turn me into their lunch. Aleks had been on patrol that evening, and if it wasn't for him, I might've been vamp chow after all. Who knows?

He did so much for me. Took me in, offered me his protection, taught me about what life was like outside of a pack. He was my friend, and there were times I wished we could be more, but it just wasn't meant to be.

I still don't want to hurt him, though. And, since he's come back to Muncie, it seems like that's all I've been doing.

Now this.

Taking a deep breath, I park the car and hop out. Aleks doesn't turn around. Hands folded behind his back, he keeps his gaze on the mountains.

Accalia's up there. He's watching Accalia.

I open my mouth, only to leave it hanging open when Aleks says suddenly, "You're leaving."

Over the last year, I've had cause on more than a few occasions to wonder if one of Aleks's vampire abilities is mind-reading.

Then again, maybe it's obvious.

"Not for good." Because, really, it's just a vacation. "Charlie gave me two weeks off. I'm going to spend them up there."

"With him. During the full moon."

He sneaks a small peek at me. In the depths of his light green eyes, I see the tiniest glimmer of hope. He wants me to tell him it's not what he thinks, that I'll be with Ryker, but that it's nothing that can't be reversed.

I have to tell him. It'll hurt; to Aleks, I'm probably rejecting him the same way that Ryker rejected me. If there was anything I could do to make this easier on him, I would, but I can't.

So I just say it.

"We're performing the Luna Ceremony when the moon is completely full. I'm coming back, but I'll be Ryker's bonded mate when I do." I hesitate for a moment, then tell him, "As an Alpha, the ceremony is a little different. We're going to have this... I don't know, *thing*. Party. Whatever. You can come up to Accalia and celebrate with us if you want."

An Alpha's mating is a pack affair. All of Mountainside will be there to cheer on their Alpha, and as his intended, I can invite friends and family. It was too soon to have my Alpha dad arrange to leave his pack, and my mom would never leave Lakeview without him, but I thought... yeah. I don't know what I was thinking.

I had to offer, though. Selfish? Yes. But he *is* my friend, my closest friend, so I had to offer.

Aleks's laugh is both hollow and cold as he turns away from me. "You can't honestly expect me to show up to your wedding with that wolf, do you? Unless you want me to give you away. Because that's what you're asking me to do, Gem. Give up hope on me and you. On us."

"There's never been an us, Aleks," I tell him as gently as possible. "From the beginning, I was honest with you. I needed a friend."

"I am your friend. But can you blame me? For hoping that, one day, I could be something more?"

"I don't blame you. I've never blamed you."

"But you could never love me, either," he retorts. "Not like I wished you could."

I can't argue with that. If things were different... but they're not different.

I lay a hand on his arm, trying not to take it too personally when he goes stiff under my touch. "You'll find someone else someday."

"Byłaś już moją drugą szansą."

"What's that mean?"

"I'm sorry," Aleks says shortly, switching from Polish back to English. "I'm sorry things have to be this way."

Only it doesn't. I know that because I specifically looked up how to apologize in Polish for when I finally got to speak to Aleks again.

For a second, I think about calling him out one lying before deciding to keep my mouth shut.

He stays quiet, too, for so long that it becomes awkward. It's getting late, and I know Ryker's going to be waiting for me. I don't want to just walk away from him, not like this, but I don't know what else to do.

I start to turn, only pausing when Aleks says softly, "The townhouse."

"What?"

"The property that Roman let your wolf buy. The

townhouse off of Oak Road? Is that where you'll be returning to?"

"Um. That's what Ryker wants."

"Fajnie. Fine. I'll make sure all of your belongings are moved there during the full moon. That way you won't have to come back to the apartment again."

I gasp. Can't help it, either.

He just... he's not even giving me the chance to salvage this relationship, is he? No chance to come back and see him, maybe talk to him. He's just kicking my ass right out of the apartment.

A growl starts low in my throat. I've been trying to be good about this. Trying to take his feelings into account when, all along, he's shown me that mine *don't* if it goes against what he wants.

But whether he deserves to see the back of me or not, I'm not going to let him get the last word like that.

"You know, you told me once that if all we could be was friends, that you were fine with it. I believed you, Aleks."

"I guess sometimes you can't tell when someone is lying to you after all."

Huh. Look at that.

He gets the last word after all.

Ryker is waiting for me on his porch. As soon as I pull up outside of the townhouse, he jogs down the sidewalk, nostrils flaring when he catches the hint of Aleks's scent on my skin.

I jut my chin, daring him to say anything. By tomorrow night, so long as we can pull this off, we'll be fully bonded. I made my choice. As jealous a male as my intended is, I'm not going to let him begrudge me a goodbye pat to my friend. That'll just start our mating out on a sore paw.

Because we're doing this, one way or another. My bags are packed, I have everything I need, and I'm ready to do this. Even if we can't figure out how to arrange the public part of a Luna Ceremony with only twenty-four hours' notice, I still plan on bonding him to me during the full moon. I'll deal with the fall-out of going against pack tradition later if I have to, but now that I've made up my mind, nothing's going to stop me from finally making Ryker Wolfson mine.

What can I say? I'm determined like that.

He glances at the three oversized bags I've stuffed into the back of my Jeep. "I thought you were moving into the townhouse, not the cabin."

"Ha, ha," I say dryly. "Funny. If you think that's all the stuff I have, you're gonna be shocked when you see how much Aleks is going to move into your place while we're gone."

Ryker was just climbing into the passenger seat

when he pauses, ass inches away from the leather. "What was that?"

I shake my head. "Nothing. Don't worry about it. Now come on. Let's go."

He plops down, but if I thought he'd drop it because I told him to, I was sorely mistaken. "No. Really. What happened? I know we talked about you moving into the townhouse, but Filan's gonna bring your stuff over? Shit, sweetheart. Did he kick you out?"

Not specifically.

"No. I told him that we were heading to Accalia to complete our bonding tomorrow and that, when I'm back, you wanted me to come stay at the townhouse. He offered to help me move."

"Then what—"

I've told him enough. As my partner, I grudgingly accept that I can't cut him off. I can't just refuse to communicate with him. But, the way I see it, I gave him the Cliff's Notes version of what went down with me and Aleks. I did my mate-ly duty.

"It is what it is." I pull away from the curb. "But I don't want to talk about it anymore."

"Gemma—"

"Nope, nope, nope. Not tonight." My tone turns sing-songy. It's either that or I snap at him, and even if he's being pushy, he doesn't deserve that. "Drop it, you better drop it."

He sneaks a peek at me, a crooked grin making him so undeniably irresistible.

He doesn't have to say anything. That grin does all the talking for him. Sure, his wolf got the better of him when he scented Aleks on me, but if there's one thing that's clear, it's that for the countless time I chose him. I've packed up enough stuff to stay in Accalia for the next week or so as we planned, I'm promising myself to him tomorrow night beneath the full moon, and I'm making my own den with him in Muncie as soon as our honeymoon is over.

He won. I won, too, since I get to spend the rest of my life with Ryker Wolfson. A devoted, sexy, determined alpha who drives me crazy, but who I love more than anything else.

Still, I can't let him think that, just because I adore him, he'll get away with being that damn smug. If his grin can get his message across, so can my finger.

I shoot him the middle one.

Ryker laughs. "Don't tempt me, sweetheart. It's a long ride up to Accalia. I already know we can make it work in the backseat of your Jeep."

I snort, taking the next turn that will lead us out of Muncie. "You're such a horndog."

"Of course I am. When my mate is as sexy as you are? If you had any idea how often I have to fight the urge to mount you, you'd run away screaming."

Gripping the steering wheel, I look at him. I have a

tease halfway to my lips—something along the lines of "you make me scream half the time anyway, what's the difference?"—when I see that a few noticeable lines are furrowing his brow.

Worry lines.

Huh.

That's new.

13

I swallow the tease, then try not to sound too concerned when I ask, "Hey... you okay?"

"I'm fine. Why?"

Ryker's hand is clasped around the bar that frames my open Jeep Wrangler. Because my wolf can't stand to be contained inside of an enclosed vehicle, there's no roof, no windows, only a solid bar that I could hang a tarp on to protect the seats. And he's clutching it like it's a freaking lifeline.

If I didn't know any better, I'd think he was nervous.

But why? I'm a good driver, I keep my distance from the cars around me, and I'm only going five miles over the speed limit. We're wolves. We live for speed. If anything, he should be pointing out that I'm going too slow.

Hmm. Up ahead, there's an intersection. The Honda in front of me takes it easily, but the traffic light has gone from green to yellow. In a split second, it'll be red. I jam my boot down on the gas, zooming through the intersection just as the color shifts.

I flare my nostrils.

I'll give him credit for his control. Most shifters wouldn't even notice the slight tang to his scent, the nerves slipping out just past what he can contain.

Huh.

Tapping my brakes lightly, slowing my Jeep down so that I'm actually hitting the speed limit, I shrug. "Okay. Just checking."

He looks at me out of the corner of his eye. The faint worry lines are even more noticeable as he narrows his gaze at me suspiciously. "Mm-hmm."

I give him an innocent smile. "What?"

"Don't 'what' me, Gemma. I'm fine. I've been in a car before, you know."

"I didn't say anything," I point out. I don't have to. His nervous scent gives him away, and that's not all. Taking one hand from my steering wheel, I tap the bar on my side. "But you might want to retract your claws. Way you're going, you'll slice right through that metal bar you're clinging to."

Ryker's head shoots toward the bar, finally noticing his death grip on it. He's squeezing it so tightly, his shifter strength is actually bending it out of shape, and that's nothing compared to the points of his razor-sharp claws digging into the frame.

He relaxes his grip, dropping his hand into his lap. He glances my way again. I expect him to try to cover up his unease, maybe mumble an apology for messing up my Jeep. But he doesn't.

Instead, he says, "Two hands on the wheel if you don't mind, Gemma."

Oh, yeah. Something's up with him, all right.

It wasn't really an order, I decide. More of a request. And, honestly, even if it *was* an order, my mate's spooked. Taking my hand from the bar, I slap it back on the steering wheel.

"Better?"

"Yeah. Thanks."

A request and a 'thanks'? "You sure you're okay?"

Ryker sets his jaw. His fingers are folded into a fist in his lap, almost like he's fighting the urge to grab for his bar again. "Will be fine once we get up to Accalia."

"I'm a good driver, you know," I say. The traffic has thinned out a little now that we've left downtown Muncie behind. The urban sprawl has become more rural as we hit the dirt roads that mark the separation between the Fang City and pack territory. "Made it all the way from Lakeview to Mountainside in one piece."

"It's not that."

"Then what is it?"

Ryker shrugs, slinking against his seat. I can see

him flexing his right hand, like he wants to grab for the bar again but doesn't want to give me the satisfaction of calling him out on it.

Ah, Luna.

It's one thing to tease him. To poke him. To needle him. You're supposed to be able to tease the male you love, right? But as hotheaded and reckless and impulsive as I can be, I don't ever want to be knowingly cruel. If something is bothering Ryker, I have to be considerate. Poking fun at him? That's not considerate.

As the Alpha, he seems untouchable. Unflappable, too. The only time I've ever seen emotion rule him is when he's horny or angry.

Uncomfortable is a new one for him—and for me.

So, gentling my voice as I turn up the mountain path as slowly as I can without offending him, I ask, "Would you rather drive?"

Alphas like control. It's just part of who we are. In fact, it's why I own my car in the first place. Like any full-blooded shifter, I'd rather run if given the choice, but sometimes I don't get that choice. Knowing that I have another mode of transportation, a way to escape... that's how I hold onto my control.

I figure that I've hit the nail on the head when Ryker looks at the wheel again with a slightly wistful expression—but then he shakes his head. "Better not."

"You sure?"

"Yeah. I... I don't know how. I usually rely on my

wolf to get me around, so I guess I just never bothered learning how to drive a car. My dad knew, and when I became Alpha, I rarely had to leave Accalia."

For a few seconds, I'm quiet, letting his confession wash over me. It doesn't matter that he can't drive. Especially in such an urban city, I know tons of people in Muncie who don't, and it was the same back in Lakeview. Like Mountainside, we had communal vehicles kept in the pack garage. Every packmate could borrow one if they need to. I only had my own because my dad figured that, as a repressed alpha, it would make life easier for me.

But that's me. Ryker never had to hide what he was. He grew up the only son of the Mountainside Pack's Alpha, and when Henry Wolfson died suddenly two Decembers ago, he always knew he'd follow him into the position. Ryker is beloved in Accalia. No one would dare to challenge him.

Not even his former Beta.

Because while Shane is desperate to become an Alpha, even he knew better than to face him head-on. Nope. He was a slimy, sneaky, two-faced bastard who acted like his loyal friend and right-hand wolf while secretly plotting against Ryker.

Ugh. I really hate that guy, and apart from all of the other reasons why I'm looking forward to performing the Luna Ceremony with Ryker, knowing that I'm taking away his only option by bonding myself to his former Alpha tomorrow night is just the right amount of poetic justice. When he finds out—because I have no illusions that he won't sooner or later—he's gonna freak.

Heh.

Good.

"You know," I say after a moment. "I'll teach you. I mean, if you want me to. If you're going to be coming to see me in Muncie, it might be helpful to know how."

I wait to see if he's going to shut me down. Though Ryker is seemingly on board with the whole "Gem stays in Muncie" plan right now, I'd be a dingus to believe he's not going to try to do anything in his power to convince me to relocate entirely to Accalia.

But he doesn't.

He actually smiles—a real smile, not a smug smirk —before he says, "I'd like that."

I shouldn't be so surprised. Ever since I said yes, he's been a lot more agreeable.

I really, really like that.

I return his smile. "It's a date."

Ryker's husky laugh warms me all the way to my toes. "I'm gonna be bonding you to me tomorrow night beneath the Luna and here you are, still planning dates like it's the beginning of our courtship. Shit. I got this whole mating thing backward, didn't I?"

I let go of the steering wheel with my right hand. I know that made him a little nervous before, but he doesn't seem to mind when my hand lands on his thigh, giving it a quick squeeze. "If you ask me, you did it just right. Well. Except for the whole rejecting me thing. *Twice.*"

Ryker lets out a mock growl at my blatant tease.

I laugh, feeling freer and more light-hearted than I have in a long time. "Hey. You gotta admit you walked right into that one."

"Yeah, yeah. But only if you admit that it was one colossal misunderstanding. You're mine, Gemma. Always have been. Always will be."

"Fine. I'll admit it, if you promise there won't be any other 'misunderstandings' like that."

Ryker lays his hand over mine, keeping it pressed to his thick thigh. "You got a deal, sweetheart."

We drive the rest of the way up the mountain just like that. And though Ryker felt better earlier when I had both hands on the wheel, he seems just as content with my hand where it is now.

WE HEAD TO HIS CABIN.

Not the Alpha cabin; for all the rituals and the ceremonies and the traditions that I willfully ignore, not stepping foot inside of the Alpha cabin until we're mated is one I stubbornly cling to. And though I have less-than-pleasant memories when it comes to the single time I was inside Ryker's personal territory, I look forward to making better ones.

Before he took over for his father, Ryker had his own cabin. It's a single floor, rustic structure with dark wood siding and a wraparound porch. From experience, I know that the single floor refers to what's above the ground. Though it's not obvious from the outside, Ryker's cabin has a basement.

Claws crossed that—after tomorrow—he'll never, ever have to use it again.

I have to park about fifty feet away from the cabin. His confession about never driving makes more sense when I notice that his cabin is set further back into the woods that cover this part of Accalia. I had to go the long way round to even reach his cabin, and thank the Luna my baby is a Jeep 'cause I have to go off-road even to reach the clearing where I can keep my car.

Once I kill the engine, Ryker hops out. He starts to reach into the back of the Jeep.

"I got it," I tell him.

The cozy camaraderie we shared during the car ride seems to evaporate in an instant. His lips thin, and I see that my old pal Duke's starting to bulge a bit against his neck.

"Gemma. Please."

I open my mouth to argue—then close it without a single word.

All right.

If there's one thing I know, it's that our mating's going to be a give and take. Sometimes I'll have to go against my own instincts, just like how Ryker goes against his every time I remind him that I'm also an alpha and I can take care of myself.

Can I bring my suitcases into his cabin myself? Of course I can. But will it kill me to let Ryker do it?

"Okay. Sure."

His dark gold eyes seem to flare a bit, as if he can't believe I'm willing to give in so quickly. At its face value, it's just my intended mate offering to carry my luggage for me. Deeper down, though, this is Ryker's alpha nature seeping out, eager to show he's a capable mate.

Give and take, Gem. I don't always have to be tough. I can accept help even if *my* stubborn wolf knows that we can handle it.

I brought three bags with me. I purposely reach for the smallest one, letting Ryker take the two largest ones.

The last time I was here, I spent most of my time locked in his basement. Walking into the cabin, the door to the basement is built along the far wall of the front room, off the living room. I give it a nasty look, then head for the hall.

During the ride, he explained the layout of his cabin. He purposely avoided mentioning the basement for obvious reasons, but he told me how he has five rooms built into the space: a kitchen, the front room, a bedroom, a full bathroom, and a cozy living room with a fireplace.

Ryker takes the third bag off of me. "I'll go drop these off in the bedroom."

Hmm. Since my last trip into Accalia was a quick drop-off, this is only my second time in Ryker's cabin. We haven't had sex in his bed yet, a situation I'm more than ready to rectify.

I lay my hand on his arm, giving his bicep a squeeze. "You want me to come with you?"

He drops his head, stealing a quick kiss. "I'd love that, but don't think I didn't hear your stomach grumbling the way up here. If we're going to have a practice run for tomorrow night, I've got to get some food in you first."

I tilt my head, inviting him to nip at my lips again. When he does, I smile against him, then pull back. "Sounds good to me."

"Be right back," he promises, then heads down the hall.

I watch his tight ass go, stifling my moan. I almost want to follow him, but he has a point. Shifters have ravenous appetites. Food. Sex. It doesn't matter. I'm hungry right now, and if I get into bed with him, there's a good chance I'm not leaving it again until I'm forced to when we meet with some of the packmates starting tomorrow.

He's gone for longer than it should take to toss my bags into the bedroom. Weird. After a few minutes, I head into the kitchen. It's probably better for me to whip up something to eat and, after a quick search, I discover that his fridge is full of a bunch of Tupperware. From the quality of the meals inside of them, it looks like some of his packmates have taken it upon themselves to provide us with some food ahead of our mating.

Nice.

I grab one that contains enough lasagna to satisfy even me and Ryker, then nuke it in his microwave. I portion it out on two plates that I find in one of his top cabinets, then bring them with me back into the hall.

Huh. Still no sign of Ryker.

Instead of calling out for him, asking him what's taking so long, I drift back toward the living room. From the last time I was here, I remember the mantle with its fireplace, the leather couch, and a coffee table that's made of sturdy wood instead of the glass like Aleks's. It's far cozier than the kitchen, and the perfect place to eat our meal.

As soon as I set the steaming plates down, I glance around. Something... something seems different. And, okay. I was only in this room for a few minutes at the most, but even my wolf is trying to get my attention by rising up from her haunches.

Following her lead, I get up and approach the

grated fireplace. There's no fire in there—obviously, since Ryker's been out of town—but that's not what she wants me to look at.

Nope. She's whining toward the pictures that cover the wall above the mantle.

There are about twelve photos, all different shapes and sizes, hanging haphazardly on the wall so that it's more of a collage than a line of photos. I see a couple that feature Ryker as a pup, a few with him and his dad, his mom, and even a single photo of Ryker and Shane laughing together.

But that's not all.

"Gemma. Here you are. I smelled food so I—" He stops short when he sees me standing in front of the mantle, staring at his photos. "What are you looking at?"

I can't even bring myself to answer him with words. I just point.

"Oh."

Right. Oh.

It's not even the picture of Shane and Ryker I'm staring at. I always got the idea that Shane's betrayal hurt all the more because he was Ryker's best friend as well as the pack Beta. The photo was a reminder of a time when they were still friends, and if he hasn't brought himself to take it down yet, I get it. This is his personal space, where he can be Ryker Wolfson, and not just Mountainside's Alpha.

But the other two...

When I was last in here, I was poisoned by mercury, feeling the effects of the moon fever, and blindly following Shane Loup through Ryker's house. Still, I couldn't help but marvel at how I was inside of Ryker's territory for the first time. Though it was probably stupid, I stopped in the living room and looked at the pictures hanging over Ryker's mantle.

Last time, there were two empty nails still buried in the wall. It was like someone had purposely removed two picture frames from their place, but they've been replaced since then.

I swallow, turning just enough that I can get a look at his face. His expression has gone neutral, as if he's not sure what my reaction to the pictures will be.

I struggle to keep control as I lift a finger, pointing at them. "These weren't here when I was locked in the basement with you. Were they?"

Ryker shakes his head slowly. "I noticed when the Luna was gone that they were missing. After everything came out about Shane, I realized that he took them. I had them reprinted and replaced since then."

I don't ask why Shane would've taken them down. I can't think of at least two different reasons that he would. One: he brought them back to my bio-dad for some reason. Two: he kept them for himself, and I try not to think about that one 'cause it's definitely the creepy option. And, three: that he couldn't risk my discovering that Ryker had pictures of me hanging in his cabin while he was still trying to convince me that Ryker chose Trish Danvers instead.

Besides, it doesn't matter why they were gone. The fact that he replaced them tells me more about his feelings for me than he ever could with words.

Still, there's one thing I have to know.

"Did you take these pictures?" When he nods, I have to ask, "*When*?"

Because I can tell you one thing. I most definitely didn't pose for them. They're candid shots, and not all that recent.

The one toward the left shows a much younger Gem. I was gangly, even flatter in the chest than I am now, with my blonde hair pulled into a wisp of a ponytail. I've got on an oversized shirt, the hallmark for after a shift.

I remember that night. I was a baby at seventeen, only two years after I first met Ryker. It was at one of the Alpha gatherings, one where a few of the Alphas' guests went on a small, impulsive run one evening. It wasn't as impactful for me and my feelings for Ryker as the one where we ran all night when I was twenty-two, but still.

The other photo? It's from last year. The pale pink sundress I'm wearing is the one I had on the day I drove into Accalia, shortly after our intended mating was arranged between Lakeview and Mountainside.

My hair was done in curls, windswept from the long drive, and there's a glow to my expression as I glance over my shoulder at the camera.

I had no idea that anyone was taking my picture at the time. I'd just crossed into Ryker's territory, eager to greet my intended for the first time in front of his pack, but I'd stepped out of my Jeep only to be greeted by Shane. He told me that Ryker was busy with his council, but he'd come to see me as soon as he was free.

I had... sensed something, though. As Shane introduced himself, I stole a look behind me—and now that moment in time is immortalized in the picture hanging on Ryker's wall.

Ryker hesitates for a moment before he steps into me. Looping his arms around me, he waits to see if I'm going to shove him away. When I don't—when I can't —he tightens his embrace.

"I told you, sweetheart," he murmurs in my ears, pulling me up the rest of the way against him as I still marvel at the obvious meaning behind those pictures. "I've always known you were meant to be mine."

14

R eaching down, he takes my hand in his. He fiddles with my fingers, but I barely notice. It's one thing to accept that we're fated mates. That we were always meant to be. I've even found it easier to believe that he really *does* love me.

But this? He told me once before that he knew I was his back when he was seventeen. I was fifteen, two years younger, and I didn't think I was even a blip on his radar back then. For Luna's sake, I used to trot behind him like a puppy dog, hoping for whatever attention he could throw my way.

And he's held onto a photo of me from when I was seventeen. That's *nine* years ago.

I don't even know what to say. Good thing he doesn't seem to expect me to say anything at all.

After another squeeze, he drops my hand and steps

away from me, but not before tapping the top of mine with his fingertips. "For you."

I look down. What the...

Lifting my hand to my face, I notice he's slipped a simple gold band on my middle finger.

"What's this?"

"It's what took me so long. I had to grab this from my hiding place so that I could give it to you." Ryker reaches out, patting the faint lump beneath my shirt. "I had the necklace made for you. I can admit now that I was willing to do anything I could to mark you, even steal the idea from Filan."

I pretend to be shocked. "What? No way."

Ryker chuckles. "I know. Right? But I'm not a vamp. I shouldn't have tried to use their traditions against them. And while the Luna Ceremony is enough like a human wedding to give us all a headache, it got me thinking. I know we don't use wedding bands—"

"Right. Because of our marks."

Ryker moves his hand so that his palm is covering his own heart. No. Not his heart, but the marks I left there long ago.

"Right. You marked me. Tomorrow, I'll mark you. No one will ever be able to deny our bond after that. But I thought... some human traditions ain't bad. This isn't a wedding band. It's just a simple ring." He glances down at it, his lips tugging upward in a small smile. "It was my mother's, though. I know you never got to meet her, but she would've gotten a kick out of how hard you made me chase you. She always said, if it's worth it, it's worth the work. And, sweetheart, it was worth every single fucking thing."

A lump lodges in my throat. This... this belonged to Amanda Wolfson?

He's right. I never got to meet her. Though shifters are long-lived, we're not immortal. A vamp can only be killed by decapitation while my people are much easier to hurt. Silver weakens us, a fight to the death during a challenge, even an injury that's too fatal for us to heal.

Henry Wolfson's death was a tragic accident. But Amanda's? It was an attack on her mate that she didn't survive.

It can be dangerous belonging to an Alpha. Ryker knows that better than anyone. No wonder he's willing to do whatever he can to protect me, even when I don't want him to.

And now he's giving me his mother's ring.

Tears well up in my eyes. I quickly blink them back before gazing up at him.

"I love it. And you're right. Your mom would've probably loved me, but only because you do."

Ryker wraps me up in his arms, pulling me tight against him. "You have no idea how much I fucking love you."

Maybe not. But he has the rest of our lives together to convince me.

WHEN I FIRST ARRIVED IN ACCALIA A YEAR AGO, I KNEW that the Luna Ceremony wasn't going to be a simple exchange of vows between me and Ryker. As the Alpha, it's always been understood by his packmates that they would get to be a part of it, that they would be able to celebrate him and welcome his new mate.

Somehow, I kind of forgot all of that now that I'm back again.

Last night, we stayed inside of Ryker's personal cabin. It was a clue to everyone on the mountains that we weren't to be bothered. Once he was installed as the Alpha, every packmate was free to meet him in the den of the Alpha's cabin, but his old cabin awarded us a sliver of privacy.

But that was last night.

Early this morning, Ryker nudges me awake. I slap at his hand, still too tired to get up.

After more than a year in Muncie, I found it diffi-cult to fall asleep without the sounds of cars whizzing by, voices shouting up from below the apartment, the hum of the humans who made up a good part of the Fang City; while I've gotten better at sensing the auras and scents unique to vampires, my wolf instinctively knows when living creatures are near and vamps are definitely *not* living creatures. In the cabin, there's me and Ryker and... that's about all.

It's quiet in Accalia. *Too* quiet. Apart from the insects outside of our window and Ryker's rumbling snores, I hear nothing. And despite how my intended did everything he could to wear me out, I didn't fall asleep until the moon was trading places with the sun in the sky.

I mumble something about "five more minutes," but Ryker isn't having it.

"That's fine, but Trish and Audrey are going to be heading over to the den to meet with us soon. Unless you'd rather we do all of the planning for tonight on our own?"

That's all I need to hear to have me scrambling up and out of bed.

It's another compromise, and this one's all mine. Both females are super eager to make up for the trouble they caused me. Trish for how she tried to come between Ryker and me, and Audrey for the part she played in the pack council's brilliant plan to throw me to their Alpha during the height of the full moon. Since they're willing, I decide they could help me out by arranging all the details for tonight's ceremony.

Despite knowing that some packs make a big deal out of their Alpha taking a mate, I... I've never actually been to a public Luna Ceremony before. I was super young when my parents bonded, and they kept theirs private.

In Lakeview, we always did things different.

From what I figured, it's similar to a human wedding, just scaled down. We'll have it set up in the open space outside of the Alpha cabin, with seats for every packmate. In front of the rows of chairs, there'll be a simple podium carved with the image of the Luna in the center of the wood; that'll be where me and Ryker will stand and make our promises to each other. He'll be wearing something more formal than his usual jeans and t-shirt, while I made sure to pack the white dress my mom had made for me before I left Lakeview.

My mom is nothing if not sentimental. When she found out that the Luna marked me as Ryker's fated mate, she knew that I'd have to have a ceremony just like this. Working with one of the seamstresses in my old pack, they gave me a tailored white dress—a simple sheath that hits my knees, a row of pearls along the neckline—as a mating gift.

And maybe I inherited a touch of that sentimentality from my mom. Because, even after I believed that Ryker had rejected me, I held onto that dress.

For the longest time, I hid it in the back of my closet at my apartment in Muncie. When we decided to go ahead with the bonding during this full moon, I packed it and now, after more than a year and a half, I'll finally get to wear it.

I've got the dress. I've got the logistics about tonight down.

Does that mean that I want to deal with the details? Of figuring out if there's a seating plan or where exactly we're going to place the podium or, I don't know, if we're supposed to provide food or something for the pack when it's over?

That's where Audrey and Trish come in. As a gift of their own to the Alpha couple, they offered to do all of that for me. I have no idea how they figured out that the idea of actually *planning* the ceremony had me ready to just join Ryker in his basement instead of turning this into a pack affair, but I'm grateful that they're doing it instead.

Now I just have to beat them to the Alpha cabin.

I have barely enough time to run a brush through my tangled hair, change into fresh clothes, and hightail it over to the secluded Alpha cabin with Ryker before they show up, bright-eyed and bushy-tailed.

He disappears into the kitchen off of the office-styled den, coming back with a huge mug of coffee; it's not tea, but I need the caffeine so I'm not complaining. He hands it to me, nods at the other two females, then vanishes back into the private half of the Alpha cabin.

I have to bite my tongue to keep from calling after

him. What happened to *we*, huh? He accompanied me to the cabin, but at first sight of the females, he bolted.

With a snort, I think: *coward*.

Does he think that putting me in a room with Trish and Audrey is going to blow up in his face? That I'm going to go feral on them?

Not gonna lie. During the half an hour "planning session" the thought does cross my mind once or twice —or fifteen times. They're pleased to hear that I already have the dress I'm planning on wearing, and Audrey asks to see it. I quickly point out that I left it back at Ryker's with the rest of my luggage, so she instead insists that I describe it.

In detail.

Whew. I'm sorry, but there are only so many ways to say that it's simple and white and a dress without wanting to snarl in frustration.

I do discover that there will be food served after, just not near where the ceremony is being held. Since the Alpha couple are expected to head straight to their cabin to finish the most important part of the ritual alone, Audrey's offered to host the big party that will keep the rest of the Mountainside Pack all the way over on the other side of Accalia.

For that alone, she's completely forgiven for the whole Coke incident.

And if Trish comes across as way too enthusiastic in the planning of her perceived rival bonding to the

male she wants, I can say that I don't sense any deception coming from her. She might not be as happy as
she appears, but she's still willing to do what she can to
support her Alpha and prove that we didn't make the
wrong decision in allowing her to come back to the
pack.

After Audrey and Trish finally leave, I hope that I'll
get a chance to catch my breath. Ryker miraculously
reappears as soon as they're gone, so even if I can't grab
a quick nap, I'd like to at least be alone with him.

Nope.

The den becomes a revolving door of packmates
coming to congratulate their Alpha—and, just maybe,
gawk at his intended mate.

I don't blame them. Though most of Ryker's pack
council got a peek at me when I came up here two
months ago, the rest of Accalia still has the idea of
Omega Gem: the big curls, the sweet smile, the
sundresses. I look so different that I just expect the ill-
disguised surprise at this point.

Then there's the whole "Gem's an alpha" thing. All
of Accalia knows, and I'm not sure what's worse: the
surprise or the open reverence.

It gets old. Quick.

Luckily, midway through the day, we head back to
Ryker's cabin. While the den is open to all packmates,
his personal territory requires permission. The bolder
shifters already visited us at the Alpha cabin so there

aren't too many willing to drop by Ryker's home unannounced.

Thank the Luna for that.

We eat a quick lunch, talking about everything and anything except what's going to happen tonight. In Ryker's mind, it's just about done, while I have this sense of dread hanging over my head as if something terrible is going to happen.

Not that I tell him that, though. I keep my dark premonitions to myself, choosing to needle him instead for how quick he was to abandon me to Audrey and Trish. The laughter in his eyes tells me that I was right. He totally did it on purpose.

I pull some of the crust off my sandwich, flicking it at his nose. Ryker snaps his teeth at me, but he looks so silly—my big strong alpha with a bit of crust hanging off the tip of his nose—that I can't help but burst out laughing at him.

He gives me a mock scowl before batting at his nose with his hand. Once the crust is gone, he climbs up from his seat, clearing the dishes from the coffee table.

Instead of eating in the kitchen, we'd brought our sandwiches into the living room. Ryker tells me to relax while I can. Since I made the sandwiches, he'll clean up the kitchen.

Sounds like a plan to me.

I'm just wondering if I should ask him to make me

another cup of coffee when I hear the front door open, then close. Considering he headed into the kitchen, I have no clue why he left me alone in the cabin by sneaking out the front door without telling me, and I admit that I'm curious.

Just in case, I peek my head into the kitchen. No Ryker. Hmm. Now, I could go make my own coffee, or I could track down my intended and find out what had him leaving the cabin.

I'm just starting toward the front room of the cabin, intent on following him outside, when I hear Ryker call out my name.

"Gemma?"

I pause. "Yeah?"

"Can you come out here?"

I narrow my gaze at the closed door. Focusing past Ryker, I can sense that another group of males has come up to his cabin. Four, if I'm not mistaken.

There's such a strange note in Ryker's voice that I almost want to refuse. Something's going on out there and after how I've had to play nice all afternoon, I'm not so sure that I'll be able to fake it much longer—especially if someone out there is setting me up.

Four wolves. I snuffle, trying to get their scents. No dice. I can sense them, but there are limits even for an alpha shifter. With the door closed between us, I have no idea who is out there, but I have a pretty solid guess if only because it *is* four.

Still, I can only imagine what they're doing here right now.

But he asked. Nicely, too. It's not an order or a command. Coming from an alpha wolf, a request like that is almost impossible to ignore; coming from *Ryker*, it is impossible.

So, with an audible huff, I cross the room, grip the doorknob, and push open the door.

Ryker's standing on the porch, arms crossed over his chest as he stares down... one, two, three, yes, *four*... four shifter males oozing both protectiveness and devotion.

Ah, crap. Just what I was afraid of.

They're all in their human forms, but even if they were in their fur, I'd still recognize them.

Jace.

Dorian.

Bobby.

And there, towering over the rest, is the big, brawny, beefy shifter whose name I still don't know—and, by now, it's just too awkward to ask—but who I have taken to calling B.G., if only inside my own head.

Each one is purposely avoiding Ryker's alpha stare, keeping their gazes on the grass on their side of the porch, but as soon as I open the door, their heads swing my way.

It's... kind of creepy, actually. It's so perfectly in

unison, it's like they planned it—or they have no control over it.

I swallow a sudden lump in my throat. I've seen wolf shifters have a similar reaction like that to the moon. We always seem to know instinctively where the Luna is, and when her pull is at its strongest, our heads will search for her in the night's sky the same way that these four are now watching me.

Not because we want to, but because it *is* instinct.

Uh-oh.

If it were anyone else but these particular four, I might not be thinking what I'm thinking. But it is these four, and the way they seem to be waiting for something from me throws me back to the night of June's full moon when I used my alpha howl to compel these four shifters to allow me to finish chasing after Shane.

At the time, they were the only things standing between me and my prey. I just wanted them to understand that I was on their side, that Shane *wasn't*, and that I needed to get to him before he made it off of pack territory.

Which, of course, he did. But not before I howled at these four, and they joined in the chase. Then, when it was obvious that Shane had a vehicle waiting and he risked driving into Muncie, they listened to me when I ordered them all to return to Accalia.

And now they're here.

With a smile that I can't bring myself to mean, I

nod at each one, greeting them by name until I get to the last one and I actually call him B.G. out loud.

His brow furrows, obviously confused. "Uh, B.G.?"

"Right." My smile widens just a little. "B.G.— you know, Big Guy. It's what I call you in my head since you're so damn huge. You don't mind, do you?"

"Um. I guess that's okay, but my name is—"

I wave him off. That's not important right now. "What are you guys doing here?"

The four of them exchange a look.

Ryker leans against the porch railing, tapping his foot, waiting for them to speak up.

I can sense a mixture of emotions coming from him. Weirdly enough, though jealousy and possession are some of the major ones, there's a whisper of humor swirling around him, plus some curiosity.

Yeah. That doesn't bode well at all.

Ryker looks at the other wolves, then curves his lips in a look so predatory, if I didn't trust this male to my bones, even I might've turned tail and run.

He zeroes in on the big guy. "Why don't you tell her what you told me, Jack?"

Ugh. My nose wrinkles when the big shifter nods in return.

No wonder why I seemed to repress his name. That, while I could remember nearly every other pack-mate I met, I always draw a blank when it comes to him.

"Ew. Your name is Jack?"

Ryker's laugh is a bark. I'm so glad he's enjoying this... whatever it is. "Really, Gemma? Is that any way for the female half of the Alpha couple to treat her packmates?"

"What?" I shrug, pointedly swallowing my instigating urge to remind Ryker that we're not the Alpha couple yet. "You can't blame me for having a bad connotation with the name." I point at the big guy. Don't ask me why, but something about him reminds me of that pulsing vein of Ryker's that regularly appears when I've pushed him just a little too far. "Besides, Jack is too close to Jace," I add, using that as an excuse for what I say next: "So, how about, instead of B.G., I call you Duke? Sounds kinda like Jack, just with a 'd' sound in the beginning instead."

Poor guy. He shoots a wild look over to his Alpha as if he actually thinks he'll get some help from that corner.

Ryker uncrosses his arms, holding up his paws in a "don't get me involved" gesture.

Oh, yeah. His pack council is on their own when it comes to me even if these four already have shown me loyalty.

Then again considering what these shifters pulled the last time I was in Accalia, that's not only fair.

It's *karma*.

I might have forgiven Audrey. I'm working on

dealing with my issues in regards to Trish. But these guys? As much as I regret using my howl on them, I still can't forget how they poisoned me, pulled a hood over my head, then threw me at Ryker—all while still thinking I was an omega! Like, he could've torn me to shreds!

My wolf gets riled up at the reminder. She prowls around inside of my chest, leading me to rumble a soft growl of my own.

Ryker's smile only grows. Jace swallows roughly but holds his ground. Bobby and Dorian, the younger and less dominant deltas, take a few hurried steps back while the big guy—who I'm definitely going to call Duke now—looks like he's regretting whatever brilliant idea has them coming to see me.

He takes a deep breath, then rumbles out, "We want to be your guard."

15

"I'm sorry." I had to have heard that wrong. *"What?"*

"A personal guard," confirms Jace. "While the Alpha is responsible for the safety and well-being of the whole pack, the four of us will keep you safe when you're on pack territory."

Right. Because they can't follow me into Muncie.

Except they did once before, didn't they? On the night of the last full moon, when Ryker was chained up in the basement and he was able to convince Roman to let Jace and Dorian watch the front and back of my apartment building.

I hadn't argued then because I knew how hard it was for Ryker to be separated from me during the full moon. I was struggling with our forced separation pretty badly myself. Holing up in my bedroom, scarfing ice cream and giving myself orgasm after orgasm with my battery-powered boyfriend, it took everything I had to pretend that the two wolves with their shifter hearing couldn't pick up on me moaning Ryker's name.

But now I see that for what it was. Not just concern for my safety—though that had to be a big part of it—but Ryker was seeing how far he could push me, maybe even Roman, too, almost as if he knew eventually that these four would want to throw their loyalty behind me.

Ah, Luna. That night had been some kind of trial run, hadn't it? For my very own personal guard.

No. No way.

Even if Ryker insists. Even if my howl did something to these guys. Don't care.

No.

"I don't need a guard," I say as firmly as I possibly can. "I'm an alpha. People need to be guarded from me."

"Well, yes—"

"And in Accalia? Are you telling me that I have something to worry about while I'm here?"

"Not that, no—"

"Exactly," I add triumphantly. "I don't know what makes you think that I need protection, but I promise you, I'm fine." And please, please, please don't let this insanity have something to do with me being a female alpha and not just Ryker's intended. "So thanks, but no thanks."

That should've been the end of it. I said no, I didn't snarl at them, and I'm ready to go on my merry way.

Not Ryker, though.

Straightening up from his lean, he scratches the underside of his jaw. "Sweetheart."

Oh, come *on*. Sweetheart? Really? *Now?*

I'm willing to bet one of my paychecks from Charlie's that the foursome already told him exactly what they were thinking when he confronted them outside, and still he played along with this.

Worse, he's not done.

Because then my mate goes on to say, "You know, that's not a bad idea," and I immediately jab a pointed claw in his direction.

Whoops. My claws are out. Looks like my wolf is as fond of their idea as I am.

"Don't you start," I snap at Ryker. "I can take care of myself and you know it."

Of the four, Jace is the bravest. If he was only a little more dominant, he might've been an alpha in his own right, and I remember how the last time we met, he was the one who wanted to continue the hunt for Shane into the Fang City. I'd been the one to rein him in and nip at his heels all the way back to Accalia.

He's a lanky wolf with shoulder-length hair the

color of straw. Though age is tricky for shifters since we appear younger for a long, long time, I go by his aura, putting him at a couple of years older than me. He's not as bulky and physically impressive as Duke, but there's something about his bright shifter's eyes.

Jace would make one hell of an enemy, but as an ally? Even more valuable.

He's smart, too. Instead of using my gender against me, he uses logic. "You're our Alpha's mate. If anything happens to you, it'll affect the rest of us. He cares too much about you. You're the only one he wants. If it'll keep our Alpha stable enough to lead, we'll do anything to keep you safe. We're just asking for the distinction to be your personal guard when Ryker can't."

So it's not just because of the way I used my howl against them? It seems like they actually have reasons of their own to make this offer, and after the extreme lengths the pack went to in order to capture me two months ago, it's like that offer is just taking their loyalty and devotion one step further.

To safeguard their Alpha, to protect their pack, they want to make sure I'm safe.

I don't even have to ask Ryker if Jace is putting words into his mouth. Maybe a year ago, he would've eventually gotten over my death. But after thirteen grueling full moons in his basement, and all those nights we spent together, strengthening our bond, I know that Jace is right. Ryker would go feral and need to be put down if anything happened to me.

And if anything happens to Ryker? I'd burn the whole fucking world down to try to bring him back to me.

Is it healthy? Oh, no. Not even a little. But I don't care. He's an alpha—the Alpha—and I would stand in front of him myself if it meant he was safe.

Just like he would do the same—and, if he couldn't, he'd trust these four to protect me.

Luna damn it, I've been played, haven't I? How can I say *no* to this without seeming like a raging idiot, especially since we both know that there's a sizable bounty over my head?

I can't.

Ryker trusts these shifters, too, otherwise he would've shut this down instead of entertaining the notion. He already vetted his pack council after Shane's betrayal; I'm not sure how, but of the seven males who remained, he swore he trusted them all. By even standing there and letting them offer to be my personal guard, he's confirming his faith in them.

And, well, it doesn't hurt to have someone else watching my back.

"Fine," I saw, throwing my hands up in the air as Dorian and Bobby bump shoulders. A look of satisfaction flares in Jace's golden eyes. And Duke? The big guy straightens to his full, incredible height.

Luna. He's gotta have more than a foot on me.

But you know what, though?

The four of them seem so pleased that I can't help but add, "If you want to waste your time watching over me, fine. But if you happen to catch me naked, that's on you if Ryker decides to pluck your eyeballs out."

Can I just say that I love my freaking mate? Instead of assuring his council that he would never, he just nods solemnly and goes along with it.

"Better be careful, fellas." He lifts up his hand, flashing his own claws at them. "I heard you already got an eyeful of my mate. Consider that your freebie."

For his teasing—and maybe not so teasing—retort alone, I decide not to give him crap for basically pushing this on me. Because, honestly? It doesn't matter that I'm female *or* an alpha. I'm special to Ryker, and if accepting him means accepting that?

Then bring on the guards.

Still... good thing I have no problem getting naked when there's nothing sexual about it. Ryker wasn't wrong. I shifted from fur to skin in front of these four males two months ago and it didn't mean a thing. And if I have to do it again? At least I know they'll be too worried about Ryker going for their eyeballs to pay close attention.

That's the *best* thing about being the fated mate of

the Alpha. Whether he's bluffing or not, it doesn't matter. He could very easily follow through with his threat and all of us know it.

And, beginning with tonight, I'm the lucky female who gets to keep him.

THERE ARE ONLY A FEW HOURS TO GO UNTIL THE LUNA hangs heavy in the sky and, the more the day drags on, the more I wish we can just get this over with.

I want to be Ryker's mate. I want to be so totally bonded that nothing can ever come between us. And I want this shadow that seems to be hanging over my head to go the hell away.

I just can't shake it. Especially after Ryker's reaction to the foursome's offer to be my personal guard, I'm convinced he feels it, too. He immediately put them to work, stationing them around the four points of his cabin, just in case.

That's what he said.

Just in case.

But I know him. I know that expression, and I know the way he closes down when he has a mountain of thoughts on his mind. He might fool the packmates who expect a powerful yet aloof Alpha, but I know better.

He's on edge, too. Like me, Ryker doesn't know

what we're waiting for, but that doesn't stop us from also being on alert.

I highly doubt that news of our mating tonight will have reached any of our enemies, but who knows? It's possible. And until we're mated, the threat that I can be forced into mating someone else—like, oh, Shane for example?—is a very real one.

Which is why, when Ryker invites me to take a quick walk outside with him to work off some of my wolf's extra energy, I interpret it as him wanting to get a sense for his territory and take him up on his offer. Maybe this foreboding feeling will go away when I see for myself that Accalia, like Muncie, is nearly impossible for anyone to sneak into.

No sooner do I have that thought, though, that the little hairs on the back of my neck stand straight up as I sense someone sneaking up behind me.

The two of us have barely stepped a few feet away from the back of the cabin when the shiver skitters down my spine. I freeze in time to notice that Ryker already has more than a foot behind me.

I glance back at him. My soon-to-be forever mate is giving nothing away. His lips are pulled in a thin line, arms crossed over his chest again.

His eyes, though? His eyes are bright, lightened with an emotion I can't quite place. Almost like he's excited to see my reaction.

That tells me two things. One: that whoever is

stalking toward me isn't a threat otherwise Ryker wouldn't be standing there as cool as can be. And, two: that he's responsible for whoever is there.

I take a deep breath, opening up my senses.

Like the day Ryker chased after me to his town-house in Muncie, I think: *They're good*. The two shifters behind me. They're good, and I'll give them that.

Melding with the other pack auras and coming up from downwind makes it difficult to pinpoint exactly who it is. But, Luna, I'm an *alpha*. Tapping into my wolf, I use every bit of her that I can to figure out who's behind me because Ryker seems so pleased with himself already.

And then I smile.

He knows. An alpha himself, he knows the second that I've figured it out.

So, with a voice that ripples over the mountain, he calls out, "Hey there, Kitten. You gonna give your old man a hug?"

I don't need the familiar scent of home or the booming voice to confirm who's there. The nickname alone is enough.

I whirl around. "Dad!"

Paul Booker might not be the man who impreg-nated my mother, but he's the only dad I've ever had. I am so, so glad to see him—and the beautiful brunette standing at his side.

There's my mom, a beaming smile on her pretty

face. She clasps her hands to her chest, moving just in time as my dad flings his arms wide open.

I take that as my cue. With a delighted squeal, I race right over to him, jumping into my dad's arms like I'm a two-year-old pup again instead of a twenty-six-year-old female. He closes his arms around me, swinging me off the ground as he twirls around.

My mom's so used to the two of us that she just side-steps us so that I don't kick her as I spin.

When my dad finally puts me back on the ground, I burrow my face into his chest, squeezing him tight. After I hug him, I turn and throw my arms around my mom. As she rubs her palms up and down my back, most of my worries seem to melt away.

I needed this.

I needed to see them.

This is *perfect*.

From his place behind me now, I hear Ryker clearing his throat. My mom lets go of me, joining my dad again.

As soon as I'm free, Ryker slings his arm over my shoulder, tucking me into his side.

I just manage to resist the urge to roll my eyes. It doesn't matter that these are my parents, or that we're going to be fully bonded by tonight. Ryker is a possessive wolf who needs to stake his claim, especially with the full moon so close.

And I don't mind one bit.

"Surprise, sweetheart."

I glance up at him. Well, that explains the strange anticipation I thought I caught in his gaze earlier. "You did this?"

"Pack's family. Mine's here. Once I took over for my dad, all of Mountainside became my family. When you came to live here, you became my family, too. But I know you still have another family in Lakeview. I thought you might like it if they were here tonight."

I don't know what to say. 'Thank you' just seems so inadequate, and Ryker's stubborn enough that he wouldn't accept any thanks from me anyway. He would just say he's only doing what any good mate would.

He's not a good mate. He's the freaking *best.*

So, instead of thanking him, I kiss his cheek and say just that: "You're the best."

His dark gold eyes twinkle. "I know."

He's a stubborn wolf without a single modest bone in his body and, Luna, he really is the perfect male for me.

From the way my parents look on in open approval, I'm sure they're thinking the same exact thing.

I know I made them worry about me. My gentle mom has spent my whole life terrified that someone would discover my secret and use it against me. She was so afraid that a male would force me to mate him, trapping me in a loveless relationship that I could never get out of.

That's what happened to her after all. For more than three years, she was stuck with Jack Walker, and she only managed to escape him because they weren't bonded.

When the Luna named me as Ryker's fated mate, she was so relieved. An Alpha would be strong enough to keep my secret, she felt. And if I nearly gave her a heart attack when I slipped up and showed off that I was an alpha in front of his pack council, she didn't lecture or scold me. She only wanted what was best for me, and starting over in Muncie had been the best for me at the time.

I believed Ryker rejected me. Of course I had to leave Accalia. I was also sure my secret had been exposed so Lakeview was out. I didn't even dare return home to see them, just in case.

But now I know the truth about what happened, I'm hours away from bonding myself to him, and my parents came all this way to be here for me because, no matter what, they'll always want what's best for me.

I'm ready to swallow my pride and admit that that's always been Ryker Wolfson...

I don't know how long I'm gazing lovingly up at him. Long enough that it seems like we're the only two people left in the world—until my mom starts speaking in her Midwest accent and I remember that they're still there.

Whoopsie.

"Your Aunt Corinne sends her blessings for your mating," my mom tells me. "She's holding down the fort back home, but she says to tell you that she expects to pop into Lakeview as soon as you can. You can even bring your mate, too, since the boys are interested in meeting him."

That sounds like Aunt Corinne all right. She's my dad's older sister and an omega, like my mom. She's also the one who taught me that, like alphas, omegas come in all different shapes, sizes, and attitudes. Back home, whenever I slipped up and some of my alpha side came to the surface, the packmates who believed I was an omega never second-guessed it since I was usually just being as blunt and heavy-handed as my aunt.

She's awesome, and I'm a little disappointed she couldn't come, too.

But then my dad leans around my mom, giving me a teasing wink. "She didn't just send her blessings. We've got a big ass cake to celebrate your mating in the backseat of the car."

Yup, I think to myself as my heart goes from full to bursting in a split second. That's *definitely* my Aunt Corinne, and even if she couldn't be here, I can't wait to see what she baked for us.

My mom's calming nature. My dad's contagiously good mood. My aunt's delicious baked goods.

And a mate who knew that having my family here tonight as eleven years of hopes and dreams finally come true.

Holy shit. Can I get any luckier?

16

R yker and I make the time to have dinner with my parents.

If I had any second thoughts about going through with the ceremony tonight, I can't remember a single one by the time the meal is over. Being around my mom and dad for the first time in so long is soothing to my wolf, and having Ryker sitting next to me, rubbing my knee as he talks to my dad about the last Alpha meet just completes the scene.

My mom has an infamous sweet tooth and my Aunt Corinne is a talented baker. Put the two of them together, and I'm not surprised that Mom brought not one, but *two* desserts with her into Accalia. A three-tier spice cake for the pack to share after the public part of the ceremony, plus Mom's favorite: a strawberry short-cake that the four of us demolish after dinner.

I mean, why not? Considering the spice cake is more of a distraction for the rest of the Mountainside Pack while me and Ryker go off to finish our mating in private, I'm not gonna get a slice of that.

Plus, I've hit my fill of caffeine. I could totally use the sugar.

At least, that's how I justify it to myself. Since we're all shifters here—three of the four of us alphas—no one at our dinner table sees anything wrong with how much I scarf down.

After dinner, Ryker arranges for Warren, the stand-in Beta, to bring my parents to the den. They only plan on sticking around through the end of the ceremony, so they don't need a bed for tonight; until the Luna comes out and the pack gathers, they'll hang out in the den with some of Ryker's council.

With a deep kiss and a promise to meet me under the moon, my intended and I go our separate ways to get ready for the ceremony. Ryker wants to shower and change into the shirt and slacks he picked out, and he heads to the bathroom. I need to make sure that I can still squeeze into my fitted dress after eating nearly half of the strawberry shortcake myself so I'm off to the bedroom.

Luckily, I can, and in some kind of tailoring wizardry, I actually have some semblance of curves; not a lot, but at least I don't look like a stick. I leave my hair to fall loosely down my back, taking the little time I have left to do my make-up.

For years, I always relied on a minimal look when I did my face, but since moving to Muncie, I got a kick out of experimenting with eyeshadow styles that bring out my eyes. Since it's my mating night, I go with differing shades of bronze and brown to highlight the honey gold color of my irises. A double-coat of mascara finishes off the look and, though I'm far more nervous than I thought I would be, I'm ready.

Ryker left ten minutes earlier to walk from his cabin to the outdoor area of the Alpha's cabin where the rest of the pack has probably assembled already. With a quick peek out of the front room window, I see that it's grown dark out, the only light shining down from the full moon above the trees.

I offered to drive with him, but after the way he reacted to being in my Jeep yesterday, I wasn't surprised when he refused. As its Alpha, Mountainside belongs to Ryker, and the mountains beneath his boots sing to him; in a way, Accalia is the mistress that I've always been envious of. His loyalty is to the pack first. Of course he'll want a few minutes alone with his territory before we perform the Luna Ceremony and change everything for both us *and* the Mountainside Pack.

Me? I'm not about to walk over there in these shoes. My Jeep is as beloved to me as Accalia is to

Ryker, and when I realize that it's time, I climb inside, take a deep breath, and start the engine.

Ryker was able to head straight through the trees. Accalia has, like, four roads on the entire mountain. I have to go a long way round, but though Ryker's wolf can give my Jeep a run for its money, he's walking on two legs. The advantage is mine, and when I find an all-too-familiar spot to park my car, I watch as Ryker walks out of the woods about fifty feet ahead of me.

It's déjà vu all over again, only this time? I'm not heading to the Alpha cabin because I want to confront Ryker, or because I can't find him. I know exactly where he is, and when I move as quickly as I can toward the beacon that is my soon-to-be-bonded mate, I'm not angry *or* concerned.

I'm elated.

This is really happening—and I can't freaking wait.

I only have eyes for Ryker. Though I have the attention of everyone seated in rows upon rows outside of the Alpha cabin, I allow myself to drink in the sight of him poured into a set of more formal clothes.

Because this is still Ryker Wolfson, he's wearing a silken, black button-down shirt that molds to his muscular chest. A pair of perfectly creased black slacks. Shiny, black boots. He's grown his chocolate-colored hair out even more these last two months, ever since I mentioned how I loved it shaggy instead of closely cropped to his skull. With a sharp part on the side, he's styled the length so that it appears effortlessly attractive.

Oh, Luna. A deadly predator with style and a wolf's easy grace, and this male is all mine.

He's standing next to the podium, already taking his place. His head is angled, tongue pushing against his bottom lip as he looks me up and down. Following another human tradition, he left his cabin earlier without peeking at how I dolled myself up.

If he thinks I look as gorgeous as I think he does, then I did good.

As soon as I join him at the podium, I give Ryker a nervous little smile, then turn to take in the rest of the ceremony that Trish and Audrey pulled together. They did an amazing job, considering we only just arrived in Accalia with the news that we planned on performing the Luna Ceremony the next day.

I look out among the filled seats, searching. My mom and dad are sitting right up front, Dad waved when our eyes meet. I wave back, then keep looking.

Nope. No sign of my former roommate.

Though I already accepted that Aleks wouldn't feel comfortable watching me promise myself to Ryker, I had thought... I don't know what I thought. I guess I just hoped that he'd accept that this is what I chose to do and be happy for me.

And, yeah. That's such a selfish thing to hope for, but I can't help how I feel any more than he can.

A pang of disappointment mingled with guilt stabs at me. I try not to give it away, especially since I'm surrounded by close to fifty shifters, some who have the empathic ability to sense emotions, but I should've known better than to think Ryker wouldn't guess.

The back of his hand brushes against mine, a soft caress that rips me out of my wallowing and pulls my attention back to where it counts: Ryker. As soon as I shift my head, looking up at him, it's so easy to forget about Aleks if only for the moment. And then he takes my hand in his, fingers entwining together, and the only soul I'm thinking about is my mate.

Maybe we decided to do this as one big F-U to Wicked Wolf Walker and his plans for me. Ryker told me from the beginning that I would be his, that I was *always* his, but he wanted me to choose him for him, not because I didn't want to keep looking over my shoulder for Shane or any other of my sperm donor's goons.

Just like how I wanted him to choose me for me, not because we were fated, or because I'm an alpha, too.

None of that matters, though. Not anymore.

Here and now, watching the moon bathe Ryker in her light, I know that every moment—starting from when I was fifteen and I looked at an older boy and saw forever—has led to this point in time.

So let's do this.

The actual "acceptance" part of the ceremony is very simple and, if I'm being honest, not worth all the effort that the Mountainside Pack has put into it; if it wasn't for the fact that they're using this as an excuse to have a pack-wide party, I might've pushed against turning our mating into a spectacle. All we have to do is stand together beneath the moon, and make a heart-felt promise to accept each other. That's it.

I already said *yes* to Ryker, but now I have to do it in front of the rest of the pack so that they know that I'm choosing him and he's choosing me.

After that, we'll head inside the Alpha cabin to finish the ceremony alone while our packmates cele-brate having a brand new Alpha couple over at Audrey and Grant's. That requires marking and mating and hoping that, after all we've been through, the Luna blesses our mating with an unbreakable bond.

Claws crossed.

Ryker squeezes my hand. Without words, he's asking if I'm ready.

A teensy, tiny nod tells him that I am.

Ryker opens his mouth—and that's when, out of nowhere, an unholy howl rips through the night's sky, drawing the attention of every shifter in the vicinity.

Including me. My head jerks toward the sound, my hackles immediately rising as I realize that *I know that howl*.

The reaction from the crowd happens just as

quickly. While some of the more submissive wolves go frozen, the dominant shifters take control. Four males jump from their seats, surrounding me and Ryker; it's my personal guard already getting their first chance to prove themselves to both me and their Alpha.

Three others, including Audrey's mate Grant, tear off toward the edge of the open space, bodies hunched, poised to shift as they create some kind of line between the rest of the pack and whoever is approaching from Accalia's far borders.

I remember being told once before that an Alpha's cabin is always secluded to give the pack leader some privacy, but also because he's the first line of defense against any threat to his pack. Anyone who wants to get to the heart of Accalia has to go through Ryker first.

Tonight? The heart of Accalia is right here, with every packmate gathered just beyond the Alpha cabin —and that's exactly where the threat is coming from.

SHANE LOUP IS A LUNA DAMNED BASTARD. HE USES HIS howl to announce his presence, then has the nerve to fucking *stroll* up to the ceremony as if he had an invitation, but he's just a little late.

Then again, considering we haven't exchanged a single vow yet, maybe he's right on time...

I'm not the only one who wants to tear him to

shreds as soon as I see him. At my side, I can sense that Ryker is conflicted. Part of him wants to know what his former Beta is doing here, while his alpha side sees the threat to his pack and wants to destroy it.

The same with his pack council. Shane was one of them, then he betrayed them. I know Jace would gladly go for his throat, and I doubt he's the only one.

It's Grant who makes the first move. Totally get it, too. For two months, he had to comfort a mate who was torn between her brother and her pack. If anyone deserved first blood beside me and Ryker, it's definitely Grant.

However, before Grant can finish lunging at the smirking Shane, Shane calls out four words that can stop nearly any shifter in their tracks:

"I challenge the Alpha."

Oh, *hell* no.

An Alpha challenge.

Once that gauntlet is thrown, there's only one shifter who can answer it: the pack Alpha. Anyone interfering would only work against Ryker, and I definitely wouldn't put it past Shane to twist that to make it so that he won the challenge.

How could I have forgotten? How could I have been such an idiot? Sure, Shane's convinced himself that mating me will turn him into the alpha he wishes he'd been born as, but there's one small loophole in pack law that I should've remembered.

Challenge an Alpha, take his place. It's as simple as that.

Of course, I know why it never occurred to me. Betas rarely turn on their Alphas. It's just... it's just not done.

But Shane is no ordinary beta wolf, I've learned. After siding with the Wicked Wolf, the only thing holding him back is his current status in a pack's hierarchy.

Challenge Ryker? *Kill* Ryker?

Problem solved.

And since nearly every Alpha challenge ends with only one shifter left standing, it's not only his pack that Shane can claim.

It's *me*.

Oh, no.

No, no, no.

My wolf bares her teeth, ordering me to stop this before it gets started. Not just because it's obvious to her that we're involved in this mess, but because even a minuscule chance that Ryker might be hurt is too much for me.

Too bad I can't. I'm not the one who's been challenged, and even if I'm an alpha, I can't interfere.

None of us can.

Ryker's still holding my hand. When he starts to move in front of me, adding another body between me and Shane, I want to tighten my grip but he gently pulls away before I can.

I have to let him go. As much as I hate it, I have to.

He cuts the distance between him and Shane in half. Approaching him with an almost lazy air, as if he could care less that his former Beta and ex-friend has challenged him, Ryker pulls that same neutral expression that always used to drive me insane.

Tugging at the hem of his sleeve, purposely showing off his blunt, human fingernails—no claws just yet—he raises his eyebrows. "You don't want to do this, Shane."

"Oh, but I do."

"Let me rephrase that," Ryker says, and hell if it isn't the conversational tone he used the night I believed he was rejecting me. "You don't have to do this. Take back the challenge and I guarantee that you'll walk away from Accalia in one piece. This is my mating night, and I'm in a good mood. So far. I won't go after you when I have something better to do with my time tonight. It's the best I can offer you. I suggest you take it."

If you ask me, I think Ryker's being more than fair. If he doesn't accept the challenge and Shane retracts it, then the challenge doesn't exist. Sure, that'll be a mark against Ryker, leaving him open to future challenges from other wannabe-Alphas, but he's only doing that because of who this challenger is.

He doesn't want to kill his friend. Stop him from being a threat? Of course. Keep him from going back with more intel for Wicked Wolf Walker? That, too. But kill him?

Not if he can help it.

Two months ago, he would've accepted the challenge, no questions asked. Coming off of being feral and dealing with moon fever, Ryker was furious about Shane's betrayal and willing to slice him open. He sold out the Mountainside Pack and tried to steal his mate. Yeah, Ryker wanted blood.

But this is Shane. Even after everything he pulled, Ryker still has the picture of the two of them up in his living room.

Too bad the prick doesn't take advantage of Ryker's offer.

"Take it back?" He laughs, but there isn't a drop of humor in it. "The hell I will. I challenge you, Ryker. Fucking fight me!"

The crack as Ryker flexes his fingers, shifting his hands into claw-tipped lethal weapons, echoes throughout the clearing. "You don't know what you're saying."

"No. You *don't*. You've never understood," snarls Shane. Gone is the handsome male standing there with a taunting smirk. As if he let Ryker's cool attitude get to him, he goes from cocky to furious in a heartbeat. "You've always had everything handed to you.

Born a fucking alpha, the son of the leader of the pack. You knew when your old man died, you'd be next in line. I want to be an Alpha. Either I kill you or I make your bitch mine. It's the only way I can get what you have and I *deserve* it. You don't want to fight me, then give me Gem. I'll walk away with her and you get to keep your head. Fair enough?"

Jace rumbles out a growl at the nasty way Shane calls me a bitch. Bobby moves a little closer to me, as if making sure I'm okay.

I'm fine. I'm not the one who's being challenged after all. And being called a bitch? I'm a female alpha wolf shifter. I *am* a bitch. It just sucks knowing that I was right. He wants Ryker dead or to use me to help him become an Alpha.

Yeah, right. Not even if the Luna willed it herself.

Ryker's on the same page as me. "I won't let you have her. She's my mate."

Shane seems surprised that his counteroffer wasn't as tempting as he obviously thought it was.

With a scoff, he says, "It's one pussy, Ryker. One bitch. You'll throw away everything—our friendship, an alliance with the Western Pack, complete control over Mountainside, even the chance to wipe out the parasites in the city below... you'll throw that all away just because you want to claim her over letting me get one fucking thing in my life?"

"You don't even love Gem."

"And you do?"

"More than life itself," announces Ryker. "See? That's something *you* don't understand, Shane. It's not about me simply loving her or trying to claim her. How can I when she *owns* me? I've always been her mate. If that's what you want, then let the challenge stand. Because I'm not gonna let you have her."

Shane cocks his head slightly, pulling back some of his earlier anger. He studies Ryker like he just can't understand what he meant. "You're really willing to die for her?"

"If I have to."

"Remember he said that," Shane calls out to the rest of the pack. "When the challenge is over and done, remember he did this for her."

I can't stay quiet any longer. The way he professed his love for me in front of the pack stole my voice away, but by the time he confesses that he's prepared to die when we're so close to forever, I just have to say *something*.

"Ryker, no—"

17

But it's already done. As the challenger, Shane gets the first strike, circling Ryker before lashing out with a shifted hand. Claws rake across Ryker's face, the scent of his blood filling the air.

After that, it's *on*, beginning with Ryker using all of his shifter's strength to backhand Shane and send him flying ten feet away from him.

Shane pops back up to his feet, pausing only to lift the back of his hand to his face. Ryker didn't use his claws—not yet—but the force of his hit split Shane's lip open.

His eyes sparkle viciously. "Is that all you've got?"

With a snarl, Ryker picks up one of the suddenly empty chairs, snapping the wood and throwing the jagged pieces at Shane before he throws his big body next.

Never a good idea to taunt an alpha, I think, edging away from the podium as the two fighting males move their brutal brawl closer to where our ceremony had been set up.

As if they can sense that I'm looking for any opportunity to bolt into the middle of the fray, Jace joins Bobby next to me. The two males flank each of my sides, careful to stay within inches of me without actually touching. They won't lay a single claw on me unless they think they have to, and as I watch Shane and Ryker continue to tear into each other, I'm seriously regretting how flippantly I gave the four shifters permission to be my guard.

Good going, Gem.

Freaking hell. My dream of a mating has turned into a *nightmare*.

My hands are folded into fists to keep from anxiously shredding my dress with my claws. Apart from me and my four oh-so-helpful guards, every other shifter has vacated their seats, giving Ryker and Shane space to fight. I can also see that the number of the crowd has dwindled significantly. Some wolf shifters are too gentle to watch a challenge to the death, and there are deltas and gammas who would be protecting them out of sight.

Part of me wants to disappear into the woods, too. But I can't, not when it's Ryker at risk, so I stay as witness as our Luna Ceremony is basically destroyed.

The knock-down, drag-out fight started in a clearing, but as vicious as it is, it's moved closer to where Trish and Audrey arranged everything for tonight. The first row of chairs is a casualty of the battle, and when Ryker gets a chance to slash at Shane's carotid, the arterial blood spray actually travels far enough to dot the front of my formerly white dress crimson.

It's not a fatal wound. Not for a shifter. But as Shane gargles on his blood, Ryker takes advantage of the distraction to kick Shane's knees out from under him. The beta hits the ground hard, but Ryker doesn't go for the killing strike.

Instead, chest heaving, covered in so much blood that I can't tell what belongs to him and what belongs to Shane, he stays standing over his challenger, his gaze gone molten.

"It doesn't have to be like this. Submit, Shane." His voice is harsh. Raspy. Full of an Alpha's command. "*Yield.*"

That should've been enough—but it isn't. After choking back the last of the blood, his regenerative properties healing him enough that he can pull himself to his knees, he sneers up at Ryker.

"You're too weak to be the Alpha. Accalia deserves better than you at its head. Jack promised me the pack and the bitch." He gets to one foot, then the next. Luna, I wish he would just stay the fuck *down*. "You yield and maybe I'll let you watch me fuck her from time to time."

Now, I know he's been poisoned by the Wicked Wolf. Shane's been taught to believe that cruelty is better than kindness, that compassion for his pack-mates is a weakness. But he made a crucial error. Underneath the full moon, he just taunted a bonded male. It doesn't matter that it's not cemented yet; all those full moons Ryker spent feral and chained in his basement is proof enough that's long considered me his mate.

And Shane just boasted that he was going to fuck me.

Maybe if I wasn't the female he was planning to force into mating him, I'd feel bad for what he'd unwittingly triggered. No way Ryker would ever let such a threat stand.

But then, before any of us can do more than just gasp at his nerve, Shane takes advantage of Ryker's seemingly stunned silence to shift completely to wolf.

Technically, that's not against the rules of an Alpha challenge. Just... more like the spirit of it. In most challenges, the shape you begin the fight in is the shape that you finish it in. Skin versus skin, fur versus fur, it's not usual for a wolf to attack when their opponent is still in their human form.

But it's not illegal, and all we can do is watch as

Shane's wolf uses his powerful back legs to lunge at Ryker

Up until now, Ryker was holding back. It's clear to anyone with eyes that he was giving Shane every chance to get in some hits before realizing that this challenge was futile. But, as soon as Shane slams into him with his front paws, jaws snapping as he aims for Ryker's throat, it seems as if all bets are off.

He changes. Not shapes, though. Staying in his skin, he does a partial shift, relying on his shifter's strength to catch Shane before he can get his jaws anywhere near Ryker.

The impact does send him flying, crashing into a row of vacated chairs. The wood smashes and splinters as he hits the ground hard, but he still manages to throw the snarling wolf off of him.

Shane hits another stretch of abandoned seats with his spine.

I'll never know if the way Ryker threw him was intentional or if he just got real fucking lucky—and, later, I decide that I'll never ask—but the way Shane's wolf slams into the chairs on his back snaps something. He yelps and goes down.

This time, Ryker doesn't hesitate.

Before tonight, I've only ever seen him fight to kill one time. When Aleks made it clear to him down at Charlie's that he was claiming me and Ryker's possessive rage had him jumping over the bar and tackling Aleks. My ex-roomie had his whole chest turned into minced meat by the time I was able to drag Ryker off of him, and only two paycheck's worth of Charlie's blood supply was enough to have Aleks recovering from the attack.

Aleks didn't fight back. I thought that the extent of his injuries was as bad as they were because he didn't fight back.

And then I see how easily Ryker tears Shane's wolf from limb to limb, leaving nothing but a pile of gore and hunks of fur a few feet away from where I'm still standing at the podium.

Just like that, it's over.

Shane Loup, former Beta of the Mountainside Pack, has lost—both the challenge and his life. He's dead, and the Alpha is victorious.

At what cost? I don't know, but it had to be done.

I only hope my mate sees it that way, too.

I WANT TO RUSH OVER TO RYKER, TO CHECK ON HIM, BUT I force myself to stay near the podium.

It's another pack thing. With Shane interrupting us, Ryker hasn't officially accepted me as his mate in front of his packmates or his council. I'm his intended, but that's all. Worse, they all instinctively see me as another alpha and, therefore, a threat to his control over the pack, especially so close on the heels of an Alpha challenge. I definitely don't want to undermine him, and I'm super careful not to do anything that might be misconstrued as a second challenge with tensions still simmering.

I still have to be strong, though. To show all of Mountainside that I'm the right mate for their Alpha. That I can support him in just the way he needs.

No matter how difficult that is for me.

With a quick glance my way to make sure that I'm okay, Ryker takes Grant, Jace, and Duke over to the far side of the clearing. Keeping their voices low, at a decibel that us other shifters can't quite hear, they have a hurried conversation. Bobby joins in, replacing Grant —who, at a solemn nod from his Alpha, rushes back to his mate's side.

Audrey collapses into his arms. She'd gone pale when her brother interrupted the ceremony, crying softly when he initiated the challenge, but she was Mountainside through and through. Like me, she didn't interfere, and she didn't mourn even after Ryker had to put him down.

But now that she seems to have his permission, Audrey gives in to her grief.

My heart aches for her. She was stuck between her loyalty to her blood and to her pack; like being trapped between a rock and a hard place, there's nowhere worse for a shifter. Even though Ryker was justified and everyone here would agree, she still had to watch Ryker rip her brother apart.

I watch as Dahlia, a petite female with short, spiky white-blonde hair, separates from the rest of the pack. I'm not surprised. Unlike me, she's a true omega; actually, she's *the* Mountainside Omega. Good. With the help of her Omega and her mate, Audrey will be okay. Maybe not now. Maybe not soon. But she'll be okay, and I promise never to hold the doctored Coke against her ever again.

With Dahlia's help, Grant ushers Audrey away. Once she's disappeared into the trees, Ryker says something else to the members of the pack council he's gathered close.

The small circle breaks up. Duke and Jace are joined by three others—more members of Ryker's pack council—to take care of Shane's remains. Bobby grabs Dorian by the collar, points at the row of smashed chairs. The two start to clear the broken pieces, but they had barely started before countless other pack-mates move forward to help, including both my mom and, to my surprise, Trish Danvers.

Once Ryker is alone, my dad approaches him. He's careful; as another alpha, he knows how volatile Ryker has to be feeling right now. Then, leaning in, he whispers to him. That... that's actually a little shocking. I've known Paul Booker since I was barely a year old, and I didn't think he *could* whisper.

After a quick exchange, the two pack Alphas look over at me.

Since I'm not sure why, but I don't want them to worry about me, I smile and wave.

My dad's eyes crinkle at the corners. Shooting me a thumb's up, he calls out, "'Atta girl, Kitten."

He claps Ryker on the shoulder, gives his head a small shake, and takes a seat in the first surviving row. I hear him murmur for my mom. As soon as the challenge broke out, he had whisked her away, bringing her to safety. Now that it's over and the body is gone, he calls for her, not even a little surprised to see that she's working with the Mountainside packmates to help salvage as many seats as possible.

Heading toward Dad, she blows me a kiss as she goes to take the seat beside him, but my dad pats his lap. My mom's complexion turns pink. She shakes her head, folding her dress under her before she starts to sit on her chosen chair next to him again. My dad gives her a mock-growl, then stands up, muscling one arm under her butt, the other behind her back. As easy as that, he lifts her, then drops down with her in his arms.

My mom—her blush now a vivid, bright red— throws her arms around my dad's shoulder, holding him close.

It's obvious what they're doing. Not only is my dad taking any advantage to cuddle with my mom, but he's holding her on his lap so that someone else can have her seat.

Because my parents? They're waiting for us to restart the ceremony. Everyone else is milling around, unsure what to do, but my alpha dad and omega mom have no doubt that we're going to finish what we all came here to do tonight.

That, if nothing else, makes me realize that everything's going to be okay. Shane can't hurt me, Ryker is safe, and my parents are still ridiculously in love. I take their long-lasting affection as an omen that, one day, me and Ryker will be sitting in the front row of our own pup's mating ceremony, snuggling obnoxiously while our child pretends not to see.

We'll have those pups one day. We'll have a mating that will still be going strong more than twenty-five years from now. I know it.

And it all starts with tonight.

As that premonition washes over me, my wolf yips to catch my attention. I look over just in time to watch Ryker walking toward me.

His expression is neutral, but I'm not looking at his face. I know his face, and I know that he's so used to wearing a mask when he has to that it's useless to try to read anything in his sharp jaw, his sculpted cheeks, his strong profile.

But his eyes? A girl can tell a lot about her male from his eyes.

Ryker's no exception. In the depths of his dark gold gaze, I see worry. I see shame. Like Audrey, I see grief.

And I see fear.

My big strong alpha is afraid that I'm going to change my mind, and he proves that I'm right when he says, "Paul just asked me if we're gonna get started soon."

I nod. Just what I expected when I saw them take their seat.

"That sounds like my dad. He always says he's too old to wait around." It's a long-running joke since shifters are long-lived and my dad's only just turned fifty. He used to say the same thing when he was thirty and I kept him waiting while I read a book on the toilet. As if I didn't know that he'd just run out back and reinforce his territory markings by pissing around the Alpha cabin in Lakeview. "What did you tell him?"

"That we're probably gonna have to push the ceremony back until next month. He laughed and told me good luck with that, then sat down." He glances over his shoulder. "Looks like the rest of the pack is following your parents' lead. Seats are filling up again."

"I see that."

"You want me to tell them that the ceremony's off, or should we do it together?"

Oh, Ryker. He can't possibly think I'm going to let him off that easy.

"Is there a reason you're trying to cancel on me tonight?"

"Well, I did just have to take down my Beta. Alpha challenges tend to put a damper on any celebration."

"Maybe in Mountainside. We didn't have many in Lakeview because, well, everyone loves my dad there, but you forget I came from the Western Pack. The Wolf District. My mom's told me stories you wouldn't believe. There, a challenge was a celebration." Mainly because that was how Wicked Wolf Walker ran his pack, but still. "You're alive. I'm alive. We survived to this full moon. You really want to wait another cycle to do this all over again?"

"Gemma, I—"

I take Ryker's hand. Well, no. Not a hand. Not really. Though Shane went fully wolf to challenge him at the end, Ryker never did. He stuck with a partial shift, his body hunched in a beastly form that proved to be more dangerous than a full wolf.

Now, with his inner wolf still riding him hard, some parts of him are still more animal than man, including his hand.

To answer the challenge, Ryker really was a true alpha. He relied on the deadliest parts of both of his halves: his animal instinct to survive, his alpha nature to dominate, his claws, his fangs, and his human urge to put Shane in his place.

It wasn't pretty. It wasn't nice. But we're shifters. If

he thinks anything that happened is going to stop me from mating him, then he still doesn't know jackshit about me at all.

So it's not a hand, but a paw. I grab that paw, claws extended into razor-sharp points, and notice that they're coated in blood.

Shane's blood.

I won't taste it, even if my wolf is curious enough to wonder how tainted it is. Instead, I fold my fingers over his, showing him that I'll always accept him, no matter what.

"I love you," I tell him. Luna, it feels so good to just say the words. "I love you, and I want to be your bonded mate. Your forever mate. Not in the future. Not next month. Tonight."

Taking his paw, I wipe the blood on my white dress. It's already spattered with gore from the fight so all I'm doing is smearing additional streaks along the middle.

"We can postpone the ceremony if you want to. Hell, we can blow off the public part entirely if that's better. But you asked me to be your mate. Repeatedly, I might add. I finally agreed. So let's do this, Ryker. I'm ready when you are."

He searches my face for a long time, looking for some clue that I'm teasing or, I don't know, fucking with him.

Nope.

I'm completely serious.

Ryker shudders out a shaky breath, lips curving just enough as the fear in his eyes turns to pure affection.

Pity that I only get to see the love written in every harsh line of his face for a single second before he glances away from me, looking down at himself.

His silken button-down is shredded at the hems of the sleeves, covered in rips and tears from Shane's claws. His slacks have burst at the seams, leaving them to flap around his boots. During a partial shift, the body bulges, preparing to go from fur to skin, from two legs to four. Something about the distribution of mass pushes against the fabric we wear when we're in our human shapes. It's the same reason why clothes explode into tatters during a complete shift. He's still dressed, but barely.

That's okay.

My white dress is stained crimson with blood.

Perfect way for two alpha wolves to pull off a shifter wedding, right?

18

W hile the Luna Ceremony is the closest thing to a human-style ritual that we shifters have, I expect the theatrics to die down once it's complete.

But this is Ryker, and I should've known better. He's the male who cast me a necklace out of his own canine to one-up Aleksander, and he's the same male who was willing to do this with the both of us covered in his former Beta's blood—once I made it clear that I was, at least.

The ceremony itself is simple. Beneath the moon— and with the pack as witness—Ryker pledges himself to me while I promise to accept him. Then, because he's Alpha, I vow to serve Mountainside as part of the Alpha couple. And… that's it. Our assembled family, friends, and packmates all cheer their congratulations, while others playfully rib their Alpha about the next part of the ceremony.

The vows are made in front of the pack, but the mating? The claiming? The marking?

That's just for me and Ryker.

Tonight's the night I've been looking forward to since I was fifteen. Young and naive, I looked into seventeen-year-old Ryker Wolfson's golden eyes and saw my forever staring back. And, sure, there have been more than a few bumps along the way. Me, pining for ten years only to be destroyed by—what I thought was—his rejection, and Ryker, who spent thirteen full moons locked in his basement when his wolf wanted his mate but he couldn't have me.

Then there was Aleks. Shane.

Wicked Wolf Walker.

But none of that matters now.

As soon as we finish making our promises in front of the pack, I take a few seconds to say goodbye to my parents—since they're heading back to Lakeview now that the public part of the ceremony is done—while Ryker tells his council that, unless it's a matter of life or death, no one is to disturb us until the full moon is over.

Then, to a chorus of howls from my newly forever packmates, Ryker lifts me up and carries me to the front door of the Alpha cabin.

It's another ritual. Apart from the den, the rest of

the Alpha cabin belongs to the Alpha and the Alpha alone. No one else is supposed to step inside until he's mated, and then that honor goes to the female who creates the Alpha couple with him.

Only... I'm not the first female who's been inside of there.

Now that I don't want to claw out Trish's eyes every time I see her, I can kinda get past her entering Ryker's private domain in the cabin before me. Shane's the one who invited her in, I tell myself. I'm the first—the *only*—one that Ryker's ever invited himself.

The Luna Ceremony was purposely set up outside of the Alpha cabin so that we wouldn't have far to go. Add that to Ryker's obvious determination to get to the next part of the ceremony and it seems as if he's crossed the distance in seconds. Next thing I know, he's kicking in the front door, carrying me human bridal-style over the threshold before setting me gently on my feet.

With a quick slam, he shuts the door behind us. Just like that, he's cut us off from the rest of the pack. It's only me and him in here, and the weight of the significance of this moment.

A girl only gets one mating night. I'm going to enjoy every moment of it while it lasts.

From the way my new mate is watching me hungrily, I doubt it's gonna last all that long, but that's fine with me. Sex is just sex. Mating is just mating.

Over the last two months, we've explored each other pretty thoroughly, though it's exciting to know we have a lifetime to try all the kinky things I've been wanting to experience with him.

Tonight, though? Tonight it's all about cementing our bond—and, when it comes to shifters, there's only one way to do that.

Ryker's so amped, he's basically vibrating in place. It's so strange to see my alpha in anything other than complete control, though I know it's a combination of the moon's pull on him and the aftereffects of the Alpha challenge. His desire for me is so strong, it's almost like a thick cloud whirling around us.

I can only imagine how *my* arousal is hitting *him*. Considering my wolf's bloodthirsty nature had me just about creaming myself when Ryker won his challenge, I've been dying to get my claws on him all throughout the first official part of the Luna Ceremony.

But instead of leading me straight to what will become another bedroom for us, he actually has the nerve to ask, "You want me to give you a tour? Show you around?"

Before I can answer, Ryker moves into me. I shiver as soon as his hands touch my bare shoulders, caressing me all the way to my wrists. I lean into him, stifling a moan when I feel his erection pulsing through his ruined pants.

He circles one of my wrists with his now-human

hand, as if he needs to keep that connection. The other lifts slowly, stroking the underside of my jaw as he angles my head just so.

He nips my bottom lip. His canine fangs are extended; not as long as a vamp's fangs, but still sharp and intimidating. The point snags, the tiny bloom of pain almost as intoxicating as Ryker's tight groan when he darts out his tongue, lapping up the bead of blood.

"Hmm, sweetheart? What do you say? Tour? Yes or—"

"Later," I gasp. How I manage to get even *that* out, I'll never know.

Oh, he knows exactly what he's doing to me, the bastard. He lets out a low chuckle, then uses the flat of his tongue to lave the edge of my jaw. "Later," he echoes.

Grabbing me by the hand now, the tips of his claws prick my skin. I ignore it. What's a little more blood when, if things go according to plan, I'm going to be even more marked up pretty soon?

Unlike Ryker's personal cabin, the Alpha cabin has two floors, but the bedroom is kept on the ground level. I expected that. Most wolf cabins are set up the same way so that it's easier to defend our territory. When I first moved to Muncie, I had to get used to the idea that I was actually on the *twentieth* story while there were times I could tell Ryker was antsy just being on the second floor of his rented townhouse.

There's no antsiness tonight. No nerves. Only two people who have been putting this off for too, too long.

Because Ryker usually stays in his old cabin if he can help it, the bedroom is very basic and—to my relief—carries no scents other than his. There's a wide window that lets the light of the Luna inside, a single chair, and a king-sized bed covered with a thin, white blanket. That's all. No lamps. No dressers.

Just a bed.

Welp, when we've come here with only one thing on our minds, a bed's all we need, huh?

Ryker lets go of my hand. With a smoldering look at me, then the bed, I watch as his dark gold gaze goes bright. So bright, in fact, that it's like a pair of high-beams directed right at me.

"No going back," he says in a low warning. "You promised."

"I did." Reaching behind me, I tug on the zipper of my mating dress. Another aspect of this dress that I really appreciate is how easily I can get myself in and out of it. As Ryker watches me closely, I unzip myself before letting the fabric shimmy down to drop at my ankles. "And you're right. There's no going back."

Ryker swallows roughly. "Luna, do you have any idea what you fucking do to me, Gemma?"

My lips curve. "I've got a pretty good idea. But you're still dressed, so how am I supposed to know for sure?"

It's a dare. In my own way, it's a challenge.

Of course my mate has to respond.

While I'll want to keep my mating dress—even with the blood staining it, it'll have sentimental value for me—Ryker doesn't give two shits when it comes to his ruined clothes. With that calculating expression of his that I've actually grown to be a little fond of, he nods, then shifts completely to his wolf.

His clothes seem to explode around him, the tattered remains raining down around us.

"There," he bites out once he shifts back again, the impatient showoff. "I'm naked. You're not."

I look down at the bra and panties set I've still got on. "Looks like you're right. I should probably do something about that."

Luna, I'm a fucking tease. When Ryker lunges toward me, I dance away, holding my hand out to ward him off.

"Uh. Uh. Uh. I've got it."

"No. Let me do it," he says, his words coming out more like a snarl.

I cock my head to the side, my hair cascading over my shoulder. I even purse my lips a little as I ask in a drawn-out drawl, "Are you sure?"

"Gemma..."

Yup. That's enough. I pushed him just far enough to get the reaction I wanted.

Hiya, Duke. Long time, no see.

If that bulging vein is any indication, I've definitely got his blood pumping.

Good.

"Well." I hold my hands up, presenting my body to him. "If you insist."

Honestly, this is almost as feral as I saw him when he was suffering from the moon fever. And maybe I'm doing it on purpose, but I want him here. With me. At this moment. I don't want Ryker, for one second, to think about anything other than what's going to happen between us next.

So, yeah. If I have to sacrifice some lingerie to the cause? I'll do it.

To my surprise, though, Ryker doesn't rip them off of me like I expected him to. Instead, with a level of focus of concentration that has me shivering under his watchful gaze, he reaches around me, unsnapping the bra. He carefully removes the strap from one arm, then the next. Letting it fall to the floor, joining the remains of his clothes, he runs a callused palm over my hip.

"Up," he rumbles, tapping my thigh.

I'm never obedient. It's not how I'm made. But if only for tonight, I'll do exactly what he orders me to without any complaint.

I place my arms on his shoulders, balancing on one foot as he tugs my panties down one side of my body. With another tap, he orders me to repeat with the other side. I do. Then, when I'm completely naked like he is—save for the golden fang he had made for me—Ryker tips me into his arms again, laying me out on the bed like some kind of offering to him.

He shudders out a sigh, but leaves me on the bed by myself.

I get as cozy as I can against the pillows, trying not to notice how he hasn't blinked once since he set me down.

Finally, I can't take it anymore.

"Ryker? Aren't you going to join me?"

"I will. I just... let me look at you, sweetheart."

Um. Okay.

He's done this once before. During those first days he was courting me in Muncie, I caught him staring more than once. It made me uncomfortable so of course I snapped at him, and all he said was to let him look before he gave me the first of many compliments.

I had a hard time believing he meant them, even when I could tell he was being sincere. Now? I still struggle, but if there's one thing I know for sure, it's that this male really only stares because he likes what he sees.

He steps closer, thighs bumping against the edge of the bed.

"Oh, Luna. I don't think I can ever thank you enough for letting me be worthy of this female." His voice is husky, dropping a few octaves as his gaze travels the length of my naked body. "I'll spend the rest of my life trying, just like I'll do whatever I have to to prove to you that you made the right choice when you chose me."

"You already have," I whisper, beckoning him even closer. I want to touch him again, but something tells me not to leave the place where he put me. "All you have to do now is love me."

"Oh, sweetheart." Ryker's eyes go a striking shade of amber as he kneels on the bed before moving so that he's finally, finally between my legs. With a careful grip, he takes one of my calves in each of his hands, spreading me as wide as he needs to before placing my feet on each side of his muscular thighs. Scooting forward, tugging me closer, he pauses when the head of his cock is probing at my wet pussy. "That's all I know how to do."

With one quick jerk of his hips, he impales me on his hard cock. I gasp, but not from his penetration. I mean, that feels fucking *amazing*, especially with the Luna spurring us on, heightening our desire, but to hear Ryker talk about how much he cares for me?

I wrap my legs around him, digging my heels into his ass. In this position, we're as close as two people can get, with me keeping Ryker right where he belongs: with me.

"I love you." The words come out shaky as hell, but I've never meant them more than I do at this very moment. "I love you so fucking much."

As my words hit him, Ryker pulls back before slamming into me again. My back arches and he bows his body over me, darting out his tongue, playing with my nipple. He thrusts again and again, watching me squirm with an expression that I can only describe as pure satisfaction.

Then he says, "I love you, too, my Gem. My sweetheart. My mate," and fuck if I need him to do anything else to have me coming around his cock.

That's the first time I've ever heard him call me Gem, I think as the pleasure has me squeezing him so tightly that—his suddenly frantic grunts announce —he's getting ready to follow me with his own orgasm.

This. This is what I've been waiting for. Though I'm feeling strangely dazed and absolutely delicious after that first climax, I lift up my hands, framing his face with my fingers.

"Mark me," I gasp out.

Ryker blinks, as if he doesn't know what I'm talking about.

I kick his ass. He shakes his head, a little clarity coming to his glazed-over expression. Sweat is beading up along his brow, his shaggy hair flopping forward as he continues to fuck me. He's managed to hold off on coming for a few moments more as if he suddenly remembers that this isn't just *any* mating.

This is the most important mating of our lives.

When I claim him, he claims me, and the Luna makes it for forever.

Ryker already wears my mark on his skin. Until I wear his, the ceremony isn't complete. So, though it goes against everything I am as a female alpha, I look directly in his eyes, then purposely lower mine. My motions are precise. Deliberate. And when I hear his breath catching in his throat, I slowly bare mine to him.

If only this one time, I'll be submissive. It'll be worth it for my happily-ever-after.

I kick him again. Well. Just because I'm trying to be a little submissive, it doesn't mean I can't still give an order or two here.

"Mark me, Ryker. Make me yours."

Some mates do it with a bite. Some with a careful slice where only the mate can see it. But my male?

Ryker is quick. I've always known that. He's so quick, though, that he has his claws out, slashing toward my throat before the last of my command echoes past the sounds of slapping skin and a shifting bed.

If it was anyone else, my wolf would take over so that I could defend myself. But not Ryker. Not my fated mate. As he tears his claws around the curve of my neck, ripping past my collarbone, I realize that I'd lie here and let him tear out my throat and I'd never, ever stop him if that's what he wanted to do.

Just like he let me stick my claws in his chest, reaching for his heart, and never flinch.

His claws sear my skin, my blood perfuming the air. I give my body the conscious decision to leave the wound just like it is. By tomorrow, I'll have five jagged claw marks where anyone can see—and where everyone would know that I've been marked as Ryker's mate.

As I scream out his name, falling into another orgasm right before Ryker empties himself inside of me, I can't help but feel an overwhelming relief mingled with the immense pleasure.

It's done. Though I couldn't explain to you how I can tell, our bond has snapped into place. The Luna has given us her blessing and, no matter who tries to come between us now, they're shit out of luck.

Ryker Wolfson is mine at last.

Thank the fucking Luna.

19

Something about being in our mated bed: I sleep like the dead. Worse than a freaking vamp. When I'm out, I'm *out*.

I'm really not so sure why. It could be because having Ryker nearby, cocooning me in his scent, is soothing to both me and my wolf. That, for the first time in my life, we can just... *relax*.

Then there's Ryker's single-minded determination to make up for the lost year when I was living in Muncie and he couldn't find me. Since the full moon a week ago, we've spent more time in the bed—with him buried to the hilt inside of me—than we have anywhere else.

For all I know, he's boning every last bit of the energy out of me, leaving me to do nothing except sleep contentedly, curled up into his side.

Yeah... it's probably that last part.

And, even more amazingly, I still have a couple of days left until our honeymoon is over and I have to head back down to Muncie.

We haven't discussed it yet; at least, not more than me mentioning my other home and him distracting me with another kiss. I get the idea that Ryker assumes that, now that we're mated, I'm going to give up on my silly idea of living in the Fang City instead of on pack territory with him.

As for me? I'm his mate—and I don't consider myself a lone wolf any longer—but as much as I love him, I'm not giving up everything I worked for just because I let him mark me. By becoming the female half of Mountainside's Alpha couple, I don't have a claim to being the Alpha of Muncie any longer, but it's still where I belong for now.

He knew what he was doing when he mated an alpha female. We're partners, but I still need my independence and my freedom. I don't regret mating him so suddenly; I think it was inevitable from the moment Ryker reappeared in my life again that we'd end up bonded.

When it comes to Muncie, though? I'm just not ready to say goodbye yet. And, no... it has absolutely nothing to do with my ex-roomie who refused to attend the ceremony we held the night of the full moon.

Obviously, I get why he didn't. Still stings. Not gonna lie. He said he'd respect my choice, and maybe that was Aleks's way of respecting it, but I held out hope until Luna came out.

He needs his space. I'll give it to him. But I'm going back to Muncie and, now that I know that Roman allowed Ryker to purchase the townhouse for us outright, I have my argument already settled in case my mate tries to give me crap about it.

He gave me his word. I'll return to Accalia whenever he asks me to—so long as I can find coverage at the bar if I'm scheduled for a shift—and, whether it's in our bed in the townhouse or in our cabin, I'll sleep by his side every night, but I'm an alpha. I need to be free to live my life.

Even if I'm sharing it with Ryker and the Mountainside Pack.

He won't like it. Of course not. His alpha wolf nature demands that he coddle his mate, defend his mate, feed his mate, and, well, mate with his mate. As the other half of the Alpha couple, he wants me with him so that he can take care of me; in turn, we're responsible for the rest of the pack. And I'm okay with that. It's just... I like my job. The friends I made in Muncie. The ability to walk around without the expectations of an alpha female.

If I'm being honest, it's that last one that appeals to me the most.

Now that Trish has made her apologies and Shane is gone, I've been welcomed wholeheartedly by the Mountainside Pack. They love me because Ryker does, but I'd be lying if I didn't admit that they don't *just* love me. They fear me and what it might mean that I'm only the second female alpha on record since the Luna.

They expect things from me that I'm not even sure I can give them, so sue me if I want to hang onto my anonymity a little longer. Especially since I have the sinking suspicion that Shane was just one facet of the Wicked Wolf's plan to get control of me.

I'm mated. Forever bonded to Ryker. Even if something happens to him—*Luna forbid*—nothing can change that. I'll never be any other wolf's mate. There shouldn't be any reason why he'd continue to hunt me down.

Shouldn't be, but on the few rare occasions when Ryker wasn't making me moan this last week, I would catch him with that all-too-familiar calculating expression as if he's working on figuring out what my bio-dad's next move will be.

He's concerned. I try not to be. I don't want a single fucking thing ruining our honeymoon—which is precisely why I'm not bringing up my return to Muncie again until I'm packing up my Jeep.

Ryker's free to come with me; he knows that even if I know he won't. Just like how I belong below the mountain, his place is firmly on it. Doesn't mean we have to be separated, though.

Compromise. It's all about compromise.

Getting him to finally mate me was the hard part. Now that nothing—not my bio-dad, not my enemies, not the Luna herself—can separate us, I'm absolutely positive that me and Ryker can handle anything that gets thrown our way.

We'll make this mating work. I'm sure of that. We have love and an unbreakable bond on our side, even if we'll clash sometimes. We're both alphas so butting heads is inevitable, but that also means that we understand each other in a way that some bonded mates never could. Ryker gets that I'll need space, that I'll need some measure of independence, but that I'll be as loyal and as protective and as devoted a mate as he could ever want—and I expect the same from him.

He'll be based in Accalia. Me, in Muncie. Still, it's not too far of a distance, and as long as Roman keeps the perimeter open to me and Ryker, we'll only be a quick run away. I can teach him to drive one of the pack vehicles if he wants. If not, with his speed, his wolf can travel down the mountain into Muncie just as fast. I understand that the pack has a claim to my mate —and, I guess, me as well—but either I'll come to him, he'll come to me, and we'll be together.

Just like we should be right now.

Huh.

Waking up without my mate's heavy arm sprawled possessively over my waist... that's what wakes me up this morning.

Last night, it was my turn to cook dinner for us. After we were full, we retired to the living room, cozying up on the couch as we watched the flames in the fireplace flickering. It's closing in on September and the mountains are chilly at night—not that we need an excuse for the fire. Even in the dead of winter, we'd survive just fine without one, but Luna if it isn't romantic to snuggle with your mate with a fire going.

In our cabin, we can let down our guard. It's the first time in my life that I truly can, and I adore this time with Ryker more than I can ever tell him with words. Especially since our snuggling turned into foreplay turned into mating on the rug in front of the fireplace pretty quickly.

We moved to the bedroom after Ryker's naked ass was singed by a stray ember that escaped the grate; well, actually, *he* moved *me* since I nearly pulled a muscle cackling when my strong, powerful alpha yelped that something was burning his butt. Nipping at the mark that curved around my neck, he tossed me over my shoulder like a rugged caveman, then brought me to the bed. He demanded an apology for my laughing at him, and when I stubbornly refused, he promised that he'd find a way to make me change my mind.

Spoiler alert: he totally did.

Before long I was panting out "I'm sorry" as he made my toes curl. Of course, I repaid him by taking his cock in my mouth, teasing him wildly until he was begging to come. He did, and then I scooted around and lapped at the raw patch of his skin on his ass cheek.

It had to have been well into the early morning hours when we finally went to sleep. It was already our plan to wake up late, eat a lazy brunch together, and then maybe poke our heads out so that our packmates know that we're still alive.

But that wasn't supposed to be until much, much later. By my internal clock, I can tell that I've gotten maybe... five hours of sleep? Definitely not enough. Considering my mate got up without me, I should probably roll right over, taking advantage of Ryker's uncharacteristic disappearance from our bed to stretch out and go back to sleep.

Maybe if his disappearance wasn't uncharacteristic I would've. But that's the thing. He rarely leaves our bed without me knowing about it. The damn wolf even wakes me up to tell me when he's got to take a piss! So unless he tried and I slept through it—which, yeah, is possible when you sleep like the dead—Ryker didn't tell me because he didn't want me to know.

My stomach tightens, some of the old, niggling insecurities rear their ugly heads.

Oh, yeah. There goes any chance of me sleeping again.

It's only been a week, I tell myself. It's only been a week since the ceremony that made Ryker mine for good. It's not surprising that my default is to remember his rejection. That, and how secretive he was when I first came to live in Accalia more than a year ago. Eventually, it will sink in that he isn't trying to hide things from me on purpose. As the Alpha, he's used to making decisions and having them followed, no questions asked.

Then there's me. Who can't help but wonder where he is now, why he didn't tell me he was going, and is totally going to ask about it.

Just as I grab my covers, ready to throw them back and scrounge up some clothes, I hear something. No. Not something.

Voices.

I hear voices.

One of them is Ryker's. Makes sense. But the other? I can't really tell whose low voice his humming in response to Ryker's short, clipped tone, but it's male. And, yeah. I'll blame the last steps of the mating dance for the overwhelming relief that hits me when I realize that it's another male out there.

Pack business. It's gotta be. Even though we've spent the last week in our own little world—me pretending Muncie doesn't exist, Ryker telling the pack not to bother him unless it's necessary—an early morning wake-up call for the Alpha was bound to happen sooner or later.

If I focus, I can probably pick out exactly what they're saying, but I decide not to bother. I mated Mountainside's Alpha. I'm going to have to get used to our packmates demanding his time—

My fingers clench the comforter in my grip.

Wait a sec.

When we're in the Alpha cabin, the den is open to every member of the Mountainside Pack. Everyone is welcome.

But we're not in the Alpha cabin. We're in Ryker's personal cabin—and unless it's a real emergency, not a single wolf will interrupt us while we're still in the honeymoon stage of our mating, especially in Ryker's personal territory.

So does that mean it's an emergency?

Crap.

The Mountainside Pack still doesn't have a Beta so, if it *is* an emergency, they would have no choice except to bring it to Ryker. Warren said that he'd stay the acting Beta for as long as his Alpha needed him to, but it's more like a wolf simply filling the open role instead of actually taking on the duties.

Though we haven't really talked about it—murder and betrayal definitely don't make the best pillow talk, let me tell ya—I know Ryker took Shane's death harder than he wants anyone to figure out; I also suspect that, deep down, he thought he could redeem his old friend. If it was a choice between me or Shane, his mate would win, but until Shane issued the challenge during the Luna Ceremony, there was always a chance he would come back to the pack.

Trish Danvers did. Why couldn't Shane?

Simple. Because Trish was manipulated, and Shane was the one doing the manipulating. And, sure, you could argue that Shane had been manipulated, too, by Wicked Wolf Walker—

Ugh. There goes my poor queasy stomach again.

I *hate* that guy. And, sooner rather than later, I'm going to have to deal with him. I might not have the same worth now that I'm mated, but something tells me that that's not going to stop my sperm donor. As far as he went to try to get me to return to the Western Pack after all these years, I'm convinced he's only getting started.

Claws crossed that I'm wrong. For the first time in my life, I really, really want to be wrong.

I just don't think I am.

Though the Mountainside Pack closed ranks ahead of our mating, it still got out. No denying that. Shane showed up ready to interrupt the public part of the ceremony which meant that, somehow, he knew we were having one. Most mated couples don't, and the big spectacle has fallen out of fashion with some of the more modern Alphas. Though there was a good chance that we'd finally bond under the latest full moon, he wouldn't have known that we were having an actual ceremony unless someone told him.

And if that got out, what are the odds that we've been able to keep Shane's death under wraps?

It's been a week. Was that long enough that news of his challenge—and failure of that challenge—to get out? To, say, the West Coast?

Ah, Luna.

You know what? I'm the female half of this Alpha couple. Not only that, but I'm an alpha and everyone in the pack knows it. If Ryker wanted to have this conversation where I wouldn't hear it, he would've had it further than the next room over.

So, though it feels a little weird eavesdropping on my mate, I strain my ears and listen.

Something slams. Hard.

Boom.

I wince. Definitely didn't need to listen too closely for that one. Even if I wasn't awake, that would've done the job.

And then, so soft that I nearly miss it, I hear one word: "*How?*"

That's my mate. Apart from the content purr from my wolf as she senses her mate in the next room over, that near-silent demand is just so Ryker.

"We... we're not sure. But Trish—"

Trish.

That does it. I guess I still have way more baggage when it comes to that female than I want to admit to because just hearing her name has me scrambling the rest of the way out of our bed. I head toward the nearest dresser, searching for a pair of jeans, one of my t-shirts, and—almost as an afterthought—some panties. Ryker once murmured that he could tell the difference between me going commando or not by my scent and, just in case, I don't want to test his theory in mixed company.

As soon as I'm presentable, I leave the bedroom, following my bond to Ryker. Just like I guessed, I find him in the living room with one other male. I know him, too. It's the big, brawny shifter who once tried to stop me from leaving Ryker, then hauled me around like a sack of potatoes, and who pledged himself to me along with three other wolves the last time we met.

Good call on the panties, Gem, I tell myself as I stalk into the room.

20

The two males are similar in height, though the big guy—who actually towers over most shifters, me including—actually seems smaller when he's reporting in front of my mate. He's submissive to Ryker's overwhelming dominance, his shoulders hunched, eyes purposely looking away from the heat blazing off of the noticeably furious Alpha.

Ryker's alpha aura is pure fury and fire; he's definitely the source of the uncomfortable warmth since the fireplace is nothing but some charred logs and a pile of cool ash. I'm not so sure what set him off— probably should've listened a little more past *Trish*, huh?—but no doubt he's pissed.

Luna, he's fucking sexy when he's pissed.

Unlike me, Ryker must not have made enough time to get dressed. He's pulled on a pair of jeans of his own and that's about it. My eyes land on my mark on his chest and, even though I can sense the tension in the air, I can't help but be turned on.

As if I called his name, my arousal has Ryker's head jerking my way. His wolf would've alerted him as soon as mine was on the move, so I know he was expecting me. Probably didn't think that I'd immediately go wet, though, especially after how busy we were last night.

Of course, then I think about everything we did and, oops, my panties are completely damp.

Appropriate? Not even a little. Can I help myself? That's a big honking nope.

Good thing my mate doesn't seem to mind. As he breathes in deeply, taking the scent of my arousal into his lungs, a tiny smile tugs on his lush lips. However, the rest of his features are taut. Tight.

His dark gold gaze sweeps over me. His expression relaxes a fraction when he sees that, despite how I'm ready for him again, I've emerged from the bedroom fully dressed.

What's the matter, Ryker? He looks so relieved, I almost want to call him out for appearing grateful that I'm covered up. Luna... did he really think I'd bounce out here butt-naked?

Well, to be fair, I definitely did yesterday morning, but that's only because he yelled out that the bacon was ready and I was too hungry to worry about throwing clothes on.

But that was yesterday.

Today, I have a bigger problem to worry about than if Ryker made the bacon crispy enough or not.

Now, a shifter pack doesn't work the same way as a true wolf pack in the wild does. The hierarchy assigned to wild wolves is a myth, but it holds some truth for us shifters. I think that has something to do with our human halves, though I've never really questioned it. I just know that, in a shifter's wolf pack, alphas are the strongest, betas next, followed by the gammas and deltas. Gammas, of course, are deltas that have survived to become our elders; the respect they earn changes their rank, while a beta is always a beta and an alpha is forever an alpha.

Then there are omegas, a specific type of wolf that exists outside of the hierarchy for the most part. An omega wolf is kind, nurturing, and gentle—everything a wolf shifter rarely is at our core. That's why they're so prized. Being around an omega makes the rest of us better.

My mom is one. So's my Aunt Corinne. In the Mountainside Pack, we have Dahlia, a sweet wolf who doubles as a schoolteacher for the pack's young pups.

I'm not an omega, though I acted the part for almost twenty-five years. I don't need to be one, though. I'm not sure if it's a female alpha thing or if it's because I'm his fated mate, but I can do something similar for Ryker. I can calm him the same way my mom can soothe the most feral packmate.

Just being in the same room together, I can sense Ryker's fury ebbing away.

Don't get me wrong. He's still majorly pissed. Whatever the other shifter came here to tell him, it's not good news. But having me near? Walking to his side, supporting him because I'm his mate and that's my job now? He relaxes a little further.

His hand lands on my shoulder. I send a pulse of love down our bond before I peer up at the other shifter.

No surprise, he refuses to meet my gaze.

That, I decide, is definitely a Ryker's mate thing.

"Hey, Duke," I say in greeting, using the nickname I gave him. And maybe I really am fucking terrible because I make sure to put as much honey into my voice as I can as I ask, "How are ya this fine, *early* morning?"

"Um. Could be doing better, I guess." His brow furrows, obviously confused by how sweet I'm acting. He was there when I used an alpha howl to control him, and he—along with Jace, Dorian, and Bobby promised themselves as my personal guard just the other day—so he knows better than most that I'm all predator. Falling back into the old Omega Gem routine is throwing him for a loop. "Sorry for disturbing you."

"No apologies necessary. So, tell me: what's going on? Is everything okay?"

His big head swivels in Ryker's direction.

Ryker bites back his grin in time. The big shifter has no clue that I was fucking with him, but Ryker knows—and I got him to grin. Just what I was hoping for.

"She's my mate," he says to Duke. "Anything you'll tell your Alpha, you'll tell her."

Duke picks up one of his catcher mitt-sized paws, anxiously scratching at the back of his thick neck. "I was just reporting to the Alpha that the pack council put Accalia on emergency lockdown, Miss... uh—"

Poor guy. I might have issues with his real name and insist on using a nickname for him, but he has to know mine. I think the issue is in how is *he* supposed to address *me*. Back when I first lived with the pack, my new packmates either addressed me as Omega or their Alpha's intended. Now that they know my true rank, he's probably struggling because I can't be the Alpha —*Ryker* is—and referring to me as his mate just seems... weird to me.

I take pity on him. "Gem. Just Gem is fine. And what's this about a lockdown?"

"Well, we would've come straight to Ryker first, but we didn't want to disturb him... to disturb you both... unless we were sure."

Sure about what? No clue, but they had to be since

Duke's here now. Huh. I wonder if they drew short straws or something to figure out who would be the unlucky wolf to interrupt us. Duke definitely looks like he'd rather be anywhere else but here.

And then Ryker snorts angrily, Duke pales beneath his tanned skin, and I decide to stop wondering about that.

Oh, boy. I remember the banging from before and feel even worse for Duke. It takes a lot for Ryker to lose his temper—trust me, I know—but whatever the big shifter came here to tell Ryker about had certainly done it.

Suddenly, I'm beginning to think I should've stayed in bed.

But I didn't, and that doesn't stop me from asking, "Sure about what?"

Ryker is radiating heat, but his voice is icy cold as he says, "My pack council believes they know who was working with my former Beta. It was one of us, Gemma."

Of course it was.

Forget calming Ryker. My wolf rouses inside of my chest, pacing back and forth as she decides to feed off of his fury.

I don't know why I feel so blindsided. Shane made it obvious that, while he ran off to the Western Pack, there was at least one other shifter back East who was loyal to him; as much as none of us wanted to believe it, all signs pointed to it being a wolf in Accalia. At first, it seemed as if Trish had been in on his scheming until she came back with an explanation, begging for another chance. And, as much as it pained *me* to admit it, she was telling the truth, both when it came to being duped and when she said she was sorry.

Could she have fooled both me and Ryker?

"You found the second traitor?" At his nod, my hands flex with a chilling crack, my claws shooting out over my fingertips. "Don't tell me it's Trish."

Ryker growls under his breath as Duke looks momentarily confused. "What? No. It's not Trish."

"Then who is it?"

Duke gulps, but doesn't say anything just yet. It's almost like he *can't*.

Oops. Maybe I shouldn't have snapped my question out like that.

I get it. I do. Me being a female alpha makes him nervous; between my dominance level being much higher than his, and his promise to serve as my guard even though I don't actually *need* one, the big shifter is still pretty skittish around me. I just really hope he'll get over it soon. His strength is a bonus, and Ryker's assured me that he's loyal to the bone.

To me, loyalty is what counts. So, instead of poking at him some more, I wait.

Ryker's not as patient as I am. I can feel him

bristling next to me, and when he snaps his teeth at Duke, I'm kind of expecting it.

Duke obviously hadn't. Either way, the sharp sound does what Ryker intended for it to do: it compels the lower-ranked wolf to spit it out.

"It's Aidan. Aidan Barrow."

Am I supposed to know who that is? I thought I met every packmate leading up to the Luna Ceremony, but I obviously missed one.

"Who?" I ask again.

"Young pup," explains Ryker. "Nineteen. Maybe twenty. Delta. He worked with Shane, taking care of the pack vehicles."

Duke frowns. "He stole one, too. But not before he attacked and made off with one of our own. And, believe me, she didn't want to go with him." His hazel eyes flash as he dares a look right at us. He might not be the same status as me and Ryker, but he's still a shifter and, as he gets over his nerves, anger takes over. "We found this where the truck he took should've been parked."

My nostrils flare. I can't help it. "I smell blood."

Ryker nods, taking the paper from Duke. "Trish's blood."

"That's what caught Bobby's attention during patrol about a couple of hours ago. He scented his cousin in trouble and tracked her to the open garage. The whole place stinks of oil and blood. Mostly hers, but she got a few slashes in before Barrow subdued her since his blood marks the place, too. Jace's got the best nose of all of us and he's sure that Barrow only has about a six-hour head start on us. The rest of the council is checking that the two of them are really gone, and that they're the only ones. I came right here to see what you want us to do next."

Ryker unfolds the note, scanning it quickly before handing it to me.

There's no hesitation as he immediately goes into Alpha mode, giving Duke orders.

"Send a tracking team in three directions. Don't worry about the Fang City. I'll talk to Zakharov myself. Have Warren get in touch with the Alpha of the River Run Pack. See if Barrow's gone through their territory. If not, have him spread the word. We want him before he gets across the country. The Western Pack is days away by car, but if Jack Walker's set up base nearby"—and he must have, considering I'm almost positive I saw him in Muncie not too long ago —"someone knows about it. If they do, I want to. Understand?"

"Yes, Alpha."

"Good. I also want you to—"

As Ryker continues to give directions to Duke, I run my eyes over the sheet. I notice a few rust-colored dots on the back. Obviously blood and, yeah, most of it belongs to Trish. Not enough for me to worry about her having a fatal injury, but just enough to be a little bit concerned regardless.

Because Duke is right. Trish risked a lot to be allowed to rejoin the pack and she'll never willingly abandon us. The note the members of the pack council found just about proves that she didn't.

In the center of the page, there's a single line printed in a heavy hand:

You have my girl, now I have yours.

I clench my teeth, tightening my jaw as I read it again. Nope. The words don't change, and neither does their meaning.

It doesn't matter that I'm Ryker's mate. Once upon a time, Trish told too many people to count that she would eventually be his. Even after she knew she'd never be, she announced to the Cadre that she was his intended *and* that she had proof. Sure, it was only so she got safe passage into Muncie, but still. It was obviously enough to put a target on her back by someone other than Roman and his vamps.

At the bottom of the page, there are twelve criss-crossing lines. Peering closely at it, I realize it's a triple W scrawled there. A signature? It has to be. And considering the three W's I'm staring at, it doesn't take a genius to figure out what they stand for—or who orchestrated the abduction of one of our packmates.

Especially *that* one.

"Wicked Wolf Walker," I say dully. "He's behind this."

Ryker's dark gold eyes turn molten with barely suppressed rage. "I guess we finally know what his next move is, sweetheart."

Luna damn it, I guess we do.

AUTHOR'S NOTE

Thanks for reading *Always Her Mate*!

While the series will continue after the third book with a new heroine (that you'll meet in book three), my next release will the be the conclusion to Gem & Ryker's romance. They might be bonded now, but that doesn't mean that their story is done just yet.

Because Jack "Wicked Wolf" Walker has been waiting more than twenty-five years to get his claws on an alpha female—and the fact that it's his "missing" pup just makes him that much more determined. And poor Trish... she's probably wishing she never met Gem at this point.

It's okay—she'll get her HEA, too. And Jack... he'll get what's coming to him when Gem finally comes face to face with her sperm donor again.

So, up next: *Forever Mates* (originally titled *Together*

Forever, but I feel like this new title fits the plot/series better). It's slated for December, but I'm going to try to get it out earlier. My schedule between this name and my other name is pretty slammed, though, so *claws crossed*! I do also have a date for the fourth book in the series—available for pre-order now: *Hint of Her Blood*, where Aleks gets the turn to be the hero.

And, in case you missed it, I wrote a novella (35,000+ words) that tells the story of Gem's mother, Janelle, leaving the Wicked Wolf when Gem was a tiny pup. It's a rejected mates story where the fated mates don't end up together. Instead, you get to read along as Janelle chooses to mate Paul in *Leave Janelle*, out now!

For now, keep clicking for a look at the cover and the description for the final book in Gem and Ryker's story, as well as a sneak peek of *Leave Janelle*!

xoxo,
Sarah

Saying our vows and becoming bonded mates was supposed to be the start of our "happily ever after"...

For most of my life, I've known that I was meant to be mated to Ryker Wolfson. We've hit some bumps along the way, but I finally decided I'd be better off following my heart over licking my wounded pride.

So, yeah, our Luna Ceremony was as eventful as the rest of our courtship. Ryker was challenged by his former Beta, and they had their fight to the death right beneath the moon. Ryker was left standing and I was mated in a bloody white dress.

Too bad Aleksander refused to accept my invite. My old vamp roomie would've gotten a kick out of *that*.

Still, now it's official. I'm the Alpha female of the Mountainside Pack. Only I'm not just mated to the Alpha male—I'm a born Alpha myself and every wolf on the East Coast knows it.

Did I really expect that it wouldn't get back to my birth pack? I might've ignored my bio-dad's latest summons, but nothing says "go home" like his wolves snatching one of my packmates. And while I'm no fan of Trish Danvers, no way can I leave her with my cruel sperm donor and his goons.

I have to go. Without a Beta to watch over the pack, Ryker is forced to stay behind. He doesn't like it, but he knows better than most that I can take care of myself.

I mean, he still has the scar over his heart to prove it.

But when I learn that my suspicions were right, that Trish's abduction was a trap laid specifically for me, I have to rely on my belief that the moon got it right, that Ryker really is meant to be mine, and that we'll be together forever.

Because one thing I know for sure? I won't be able to take his rejection again...

* ***Forever Mates*** is the third novel in the *Claws and Fangs* series, and the conclusion to Gem and Ryker's story.

Releasing December 7, 2021!

LEAVE JANELLE

A SNEAK PEEK AT THE PREQUEL FEATURING GEM'S MOTHER

I enter the cave as cautiously as my other half will let me. She assures me that the worst I have to fear is a few chirping insects and maybe a frog or two, but I have to see for myself.

Only when I've proved that it's as safe a sanctuary as I could hope for do I finally loosen my death grip on my daughter's scruff.

She drops to the stony ground before immediately spinning around, ducking under my front legs.

I rumble, letting her know that I'm here. I'm with her.

We're together.

Thank the Luna.

Unfortunately, though, my wolf's fur is still soaked. Hers too. We have no human clothes so, for now, we'll have to stay in our fur. Despite it being summertime, the shadowed cave is chilly. Even if we're drenched, we'll be warmer wearing our fur over being naked in the dark.

I lay down on the ground, nudging Ruby so that she's nestled in front of me while I get as comfortable as I can. Then, once I have, I nod at the space I've left for her. With another of her yips, she plops down between my paws.

She's gotta be exhausted.

Laying one of my paws on her back, I start to clean her with the flat of my tongue. Not the type of bath I prefer to give my girl, but it's all I can do right now.

When she's as dry and as clean as I can make her, she curls up, resting her muzzle on her own paws as she blinks sleepily up at me.

Ah, sweetie.

My girl.

My Ruby—

No.

No.

I don't know why it's only just hitting me now, but as my wolf nuzzles the top of her head, I realize that leaving the Wolf District... that was only the beginning. Sure, we made it out of Jack's territory and onto some other pack's land, but the shifter world is small. There's no way I can hide from Jack forever—I accepted that even before I left the cabin behind—but she, at least, has a *chance*.

If I want to save her from Jack, Ruby Walker the omega wolf has to disappear.

She's too young to know what we're running from, what we're leaving behind, and in some ways, that's a blessing. Maybe we can start over after all. And even if *we* can't, I'll do anything to give her that chance.

It's a good thing that I was always so careful to keep her hidden. The pack knew we had a pup, but Jack didn't push me to show her off to them. She was his dirty little secret, the runt of an omega wolf that he couldn't believe he had sired.

And if Jack had actually sired an alpha?

Oopsie...

I peer down at my daughter. Now that he knows the truth, it's not just me he won't want to get away. I can't even begin to imagine how valuable my little alpha is, and I've had the last year to come to grips with it.

The thing is, *I* don't have to go back there. Getting out was the hard part, but since we never actually bonded, I can leave him; as much as Jack will fume over it, I'm not on his territory so I'm not under his control anymore. He can't bring me back if I don't want to go. But Ruby is still his daughter. He has a claim to her. He's her father, and even though she's here with me, there isn't a single shifter alive that would stop Jack from getting to his daughter.

Which means that, from this moment on, she can't be.

Okay. *Okay*. If she can't be Ruby Walker, who can she be?

When I was pregnant with her, I used to daydream about what it would be like once my daughter was born. There was a connection between us from the beginning, and even if I couldn't tell that she would be so unique, I always knew she'd be my girl.

Ruby was one of my top choices for her name. I had a few others, too, but I was the only one coming up with girl names. Jack was so proud that I was having his pup that he refused to accept that she'd be anything but his Junior.

Of course, then he discovered that she was female and he lost his Luna damned mind over it as if I did it on purpose. He refused to even meet her the first few days of her life, and when he finally did, he just called her "that". Better than "little bitch", but any illusions I had that being a father might change him died a quick death that day.

On the plus side, I got to name her.

And now, a year later, I'm going to change it.

I need something sweet. Something delicate. A name so harmless, no one will ever guess she's a female alpha or the daughter of the Wicked Wolf.

It hits me right as my head starts to feel heavy and I'm ready to follow my dozing daughter into sleep.

Gemma.

My second choice for a name, and due to Jack's refusal to discuss any female names, no one would ever know except for me.

And not just Gemma. To distance her from her infamous father, I also need to change her last name. As soon as Jack took me as his mate, mine was changed to Walker to match his, but even if I gave her my maiden name, it would be too easy to tie her back to me. She has to be someone else entirely.

Gentle.

Non-threatening.

The opposite of a predator—

Swann.

I'm going to call her Gemma Swann.

Who can be afraid of a smiling, blonde pup called Gemma Swann?

But, most importantly, she'll still be my Ruby deep down.

My precious, precious Gem...

AVAILABLE NOW

LEAVE JANELLE

Sometimes fate gets it wrong.

When the Luna announced that I was fated to be the mate of the Western Pack's Alpha, Jack "Wicked Wolf" Walker, I knew that I would never survive him.

I'm an omega. Gentle by nature, all of my packmates thought I could temper his cruelty—but they were way wrong. As it is, it's all I can do to avoid being marked by him and tied to him for life. Luckily, my brute of a mate has a taste for females, and fully bonding me to him means that he won't get to hop from cabin to cabin while I pretend like I'm happy to be called *his*.

For three years, I walked a thin line between being Jack's plaything and his bonded mate. When I gave birth to his pup, I thought he might change, but I did the one thing that he considered unthinkable: I gave him a daughter.

Worse, I gave him the first female alpha since the Luna herself.

Not that he knows that. I manage to hide her true nature, passing her off as an omega just like me—until Jack discovers the truth, and I'm left with no choice but to leave.

I know he'll come after us. My mate is psychotic, he's vicious, and he's cruel. He thinks he owns me, and he'll kill my daughter if he can get his claws on her. And while I may be an omega, I'm also a wolf. I'll protect her, no matter what, and when I pass into the territory of a neighboring pack, I attack the first wolf I see.

Who just so happens to be the Alpha of the Lakeview Pack...

---

* *Leave Janelle* is a prequel novella (35,000+ words) that is set approximately twenty-five years before the events of *Never His Mate*, and it's the story of Gemma's mother.

Out now!

KEEP IN TOUCH

Stay tuned for what's coming up next! Sign up for my mailing list for news, promotions, upcoming releases, and more!

Sarah Spade's Stories

And make sure to check out my Facebook page for all release news:

http://facebook.com/sarahspadebooks

Sarah Spade is a pen name that I used specifically to write these holiday-based novellas (as well as a few books that will be coming out in the future). If you're interested in reading other books that I've written (romantic suspense, Greek mythology-based romance, shifters/vampires/witches romance, and fae romance), check out my primary author account here:

http://amazon.com/author/jessicalynch

ALSO BY SARAH SPADE

Holiday Hunk

Halloween Boo

This Christmas

Auld Lang Mine

I'm With Cupid

Getting Lucky

When Sparks Fly

Holiday Hunk: the Complete Series

Claws and Fangs

Leave Janelle

Never His Mate

Always Her Mate

Forever Mates

Hint of Her Blood

Taste of His Skin

Claws Clause

(written as Jessica Lynch)

Mates *free*

Printed in Great Britain
by Amazon